The Anti-Book

THE ANTI-BOOK

RAPHAEL SIMON

Dial Books for Young Readers

Dial Books for Young Readers
An imprint of Penguin Random House LLC, New York

First published in the United States of America by Dial Books for Young Readers,
an imprint of Penguin Random House LLC, 2021

Library of Congress Cataloging-in-Publication Data
Names: Simon, Raphael (Children's author), author. | Title: The anti-book / Raphael Simon.
Description: New York : Dial Books for Young Readers, [2021] | Audience: Ages 8–12 |
Audience: Grades 4–6 | Summary: "Mickey finds a book that promises to erase whatever
is written in it, and after filling the page with all the things and people he dislikes, he finds
himself in the anti-world, where everything familiar is gone"— Provided by publisher.
Identifiers: LCCN 2020049236 (print) | LCCN 2020049237 (ebook) | ISBN 9780525552413
(hardcover) | ISBN 9780525552437 (ebook) | Subjects: CYAC: Fantasy. | Magic—Fiction. |
Books—Fiction. | Classification: LCC PZ7.1.S558 An 2021 (print) | LCC PZ7.1.S558 (ebook)
DDC [Fic]—dc23 | LC record available at https://lccn.loc.gov/2020049236
LC ebook record available at https://lccn.loc.gov/2020049237

Printed in the United States of America
ISBN 9780525552413
1 3 5 7 9 10 8 6 4 2

Design by Jennifer Kelly
Text set in Amasis MT Pro

for nobody

table of discontents

part one: *ad*
1

part two: *rad*
51

part three: *mad*
115

part four: *bad*
195

part four and a half: *worse*
239

part five: *sad*
261

part six: *glad*
289

epilogue
303

The Anti-Book

part one:
ad

1.

Get lost!

That's what Mickey says to everyone these days.

He might even say it to you if he knew you were here.

"GET LOST!"

See?

It isn't personal. He has nothing against you. He just wants to be left alone.

2.

Get lost, dog!

It isn't just people. He even tells his dog to get lost.

"GET LOST, DOG!"

See?

Sometimes Mickey has to say it more than once.

"GET LOST, DOG!"

"I SAID, GET LOST, NOODLE!"

Yes, Noodle is his dog's name—unfortunately. Mickey prefers not to say it aloud.

You probably think it is unkind for a boy to tell a dog to get lost. Unless the dog is biting him. Or the boy is allergic to dogs.

Mickey's dog never bites him. Mickey is not allergic to dogs.

Besides, Mickey's dog is hypoallergenic.

Mickey just wants his dog to go away. And he wants you to go away too.

It isn't personal. It isn't doggerel, either.

(That was a joke. *Doggerel* is bad poetry, or gibberish; it has nothing to do with dogs.)

Of course, it wasn't always this way. Noodle used to be Mickey's favorite thing in the world.

He never minded that Noodle smelled when his coat got wet. Or that Noodle always held on to balls when they played fetch. Or that Noodle made muddy paw prints—"Noodle Doodles," Mickey called them—on Mickey's bed at night.

You might even say Mickey loved those things about Noodle.

Then one day, for no apparent reason, he stopped loving them.

Like I said, it isn't personal. He just doesn't love anything very much anymore.

3.

Get lost, sister!

Well, sometimes it's a little personal. Like with his sister, Alice.

His *big* sister, as Alice always reminds him.

"GET LOST, SISTER."

"*Big* sister."

See?

"GET LOST, *BIG* SISTER."

"With pleasure!" she replies. But she never goes very far.

Alice is always telling Mickey to grow up and to think about other people for a change.

"You mean like you?"

"For starters."

Mickey's big sister is only two years older than Mickey. Well, two and a half. Which is hardly older at all, in Mickey's opinion.

Being so close in age, Mickey and Alice used to be close friends. Or if not close friends, at least close siblings. Which is close enough.

"You're my best little brother," Alice would say.

"I'm your *only* little brother," Mickey would say back.

Or Mickey would say, "You're my best big sister."

And Alice would say back, "I'm your *only* big sister."

It was like a secret handshake.

It meant *You're awesome*. It meant *I've got your back*. It meant *I love you*.

Then, one day, Mickey's older sister got an older boyfriend. Older, that is, than she. Two years older.

Mickey: twelve. Alice: fifteen. Boyfriend: seventeen.

Seventeen!

A two-year difference might not be much in the case of, say, siblings, but when it comes to a boyfriend, in Mickey's opinion, it's *much* too much.

Alice disagrees. As she sees it, having such an old boyfriend means that she is no longer just a little bit older than Mickey; she is a lot older.

And a lot bigger.

Math is funny that way.

4.

Get lost, sister's boyfriend!

Get lost, sister's boyfriend's friend!

As if all that weren't bad enough, Alice's boyfriend is a bodybuilder. He has extra-large biceps, or as he calls them, "guns," and extra-defined abdominal muscles, or as he calls them, "abs"—features that he shows off by wearing extra-small T-shirts. Aside from his body, which he prizes above all else, and Alice, who in theory comes next, Alice's boyfriend's main pride and joy is his vintage muscle car, a 1968 Camaro SS, if you want to know the exact year and model.

(Mickey doesn't want to know the exact year and model.)

Mickey calls Alice's boyfriend "Car-Boy"—or, less often, "Car-Friend," or "Muscle-Boy," or "Muscle-Friend"—but never to Car-Boy's face. He doesn't say much to Car-Boy's face, if he can help it.

Car-Boy has no hesitation speaking to Mickey. He calls Mickey by names that are unrepeatable and, in Mickey's opinion, un-clever. Most of these names begin with a word for a rear end, and end with the word *-head* or *-wipe*.

Car-Boy lives around the corner from Mickey. When he is not polishing his car in his driveway, he can usually be found loitering on the bridge near Mickey's school, where his best friend the mime performs.

Yes, Car-Boy's best friend is a mime. He wears white face makeup and a black beret, and he even has a red plastic carnation that squirts water—most often at Mickey. Mickey's names for him are "Mime-Boy," "Beret-Boy," and "Silent Scream." And, no, Mickey doesn't say those names aloud either.

Both Car-Boy and Mime-Boy like to hang out and do nothing except take a lot of selfies and harass whoever is unlucky enough to pass by. In other ways, they are an unlikely pair. Unless you imagine them as a circus act, which Mickey often does to amuse himself. Not that Car-Boy has any circus talents. Unless you count throwing the belongings of young kids over the side of the bridge.

Mime-Boy, on the other hand, juggles small, purloined objects, pats imaginary prison walls, and imitates the way people walk—Mickey, for instance. Judging from Mime-Boy's miming motions, Mickey is two feet tall and walks like a robot.

Judging from his loud laughter, Car-Boy finds this extremely funny.

Here's what's really infuriating:

If Mickey walks like a robot, it's Car-Boy's fault.

You see, the first time Alice invited Car-Boy into their house, Car-Boy told Mickey he walked like a girl.

"I do not," said Mickey. "What does that even mean anyway?"

"You know, with your hands like this—" Car-Boy demonstrated, his hands dangling limply from his wrists.

"Girls don't walk like that."

Car-Boy shrugged. "I just thought you should know. Since you're sort of like my little brother now. Don't be mad."

"I'm not like your little brother. And I'm not mad."

Nonetheless, from that day onward, Mickey has walked with his arms stiff at his sides. Like a robot. And Mime-Boy has imitated his walk. And Car-Boy has laughed. And then laughed again, just in case Mickey didn't hear him the first time.

For someone so old, I think you'll agree, Car-Boy is not very mature. He's definitely not very nice. Same goes for Mime-Boy.

"GET LOST, CAR-BOY!"

"GET LOST, MIME-BOY!"

No, Mickey doesn't really say that. He's too scared. Car-Boy is much bigger than he is. So is Mime-Boy. But Mickey thinks it.

5.

Get lost, parents!

Perhaps you will not be surprised to hear that Mickey's parents are the people Mickey most often tells to get lost. Although he rarely tells them both to get lost at once because his parents are getting a divorce and these days they are rarely in the same place at the same time.

Mickey's mom and dad do not believe it's not personal when he tells them to get lost. They think he's mad at them.

"I feel a lot of negative energy coming from you," his mom says, tying the laces of her new hiking boots. "You're not making it easy for me to go through my own process."

"I'm not mad!"

"Blame me if you need to, but I thought you were smarter than that," says his dad, trimming his new beard. "Divorce is never one-sided."

"I'm not mad!"

Why should Mickey be mad? Their divorce is their business.

It's like he's always hearing in school: *Your body, your choices.* Or in this case: *Their bodies, their choices.*

What Mickey's parents—his *ex*-parents—don't realize is that their divorce has nothing to do with him. Because *he's* going to divorce *them.*

Believe it or not, it is perfectly legal to divorce your parents. As long as you meet certain requirements.

Of course, they don't call it divorce; they call it *emancipation. Emancipation* means "freedom," basically.

Look it up. Mickey did.

If there's anything that makes Mickey mad it's that he didn't see the divorce coming. Mickey prides himself on seeing what's coming.

To be fair, his parents didn't give much warning. They never fought. They didn't sleep in separate rooms like some parents Mickey knew. They seemed perfectly happy. Or at least not *un*happy.

This past winter, they celebrated the holidays together, as usual. And that is no small thing because Mickey's family has always celebrated Hanukkah *and* Christmas. All eight days of one and all twelve days of the other. Collectively known in their house as the twenty days of *Chrisnukkah.*

They even celebrated New Year's Eve with their traditional game of charades.

Two days later, first thing in the morning, before the

Chrisnukkah menorah could be put away or the Chrisnukkah tree could be taken down, Mickey's parents called a family meeting.

They had news, they said. Not good news or bad news, necessarily; just . . . news.

They were separating. That very day. Officially, it would be a trial separation, but they expected to make it permanent soon.

In fact, the separation had been brewing for a long time, but they hadn't wanted to say anything until after the holidays.

"We didn't want you to think of the breakup every time Chrisnukkah came around," said Mickey's dad.

"Not that we think of it as a breakup!" corrected Mickey's mom. "We're still very good friends."

Mickey couldn't quite grasp what was happening. He'd been certain the family meeting was going to be about household chores and the need for a new system for doing dishes. Or maybe one of his mother's wild schemes had finally gotten off the ground—the Ostrich Farm, say, or that "Staycation" travel agency—and they were going to have to move to accommodate her new business.

"If you're such good friends, why are you getting a divorce?" Mickey heard himself ask.

"Friendship is not the same thing as love," his parents answered.

"Parents have needs and feelings too, you know,"

Mickey's sister reminded him. "Can't you think about anybody but yourself?"

Then, despite her very grown-up and sophisticated understanding of the fact that parents have needs and feelings too, she burst into tears and ran out of the room.

Instinctively, Mickey followed. In the old days, it would have been his job to cheer her up. To tell her she was his best big sister. To laugh when she replied that she was his only sister.

But by the time he got upstairs and peeked into her bedroom, she already had her headphones on. She wanted to be left alone.

Mickey understood. He wanted to be left alone too.

"GET LOST, MOM!"

"GET LOST, DAD!"

"GET LOST, CHRISNUKKAH!"

6.

Get lost, Charlies!

The fact that Mickey's parents are very good friends is not the only reason they are getting divorced.

One reason is named Charlene, but is called Charlie. Charlie is "somebody new" that Mickey's father met. Charlie is going to be Mickey's father's new wife.

Another reason is named Charlotte, but is also called Charlie. This Charlie is "somebody new" Mickey's mother met. This somebody new is actually somebody old. An old friend of Mickey's mother's whom Mickey has known for years. She is going to be Mickey's mother's new wife.

That's right. Mickey's mother and father are each marrying a woman named Charlie. What are the odds?

(And why can't the Charlies just marry each other instead, Mickey wants to ask, but of course he never does.)

Both Charlies compulsively bake chocolate chip cookies.

Mom's Charlie, who is a yoga instructor, makes her cookies soft and flexible "with inner core strength"; Mickey calls her "Chewy Charlie." Dad's Charlie, who is a lawyer, makes her cookies hard and crisp "like a good legal argument"; Mickey calls her "Crispy Charlie."

While their cookies are not exactly the same, the intention behind the cookies is the same: to win over their soon-to-be stepchildren.

Mickey will not be won over.

The first time he stayed overnight at his father's new house, which happens to have been the last time he stayed overnight at his father's new house, he refused to eat Crispy Charlie's cookies. He wouldn't take a single bite. He told her he had a stomachache.

Later, lying in bed, he heard his father talking to his soon-to-be stepmother.

"Sorry about Mickey," his father was saying. "I don't know what's going on with that kid. He doesn't play with other boys anymore. He doesn't look me in the eye. The only person he talks to is himself! I give up."

Mickey didn't really want to listen, but he couldn't help it. It was like trying to tear your eyes away from a car crash.

"I just want to start all over—with you," his father continued in a husky voice that Mickey barely recognized. "And I want to do it right this time. The whole family thing."

Meaning there was something wrong the first time.

Meaning there was something wrong with Mickey.

Well, so what, thought Mickey. Let his father start over. Mickey would start over too.

He certainly wouldn't be staying at his father's house again.

"GET LOST, CHEWY CHARLIE!"

"GET LOST, CRISPY CHARLIE!"

"GET LOST, CHOCOLATE CHIP COOKIES OF BOTH TYPES!"

7.

Get lost, school!

Mickey lives in the desert. Or more precisely in a sub-urban neighborhood that was once desert and is still surrounded on two sides by sand and rock and cactus.

The name of this neighborhood is Arroyo Perdido.

An *arroyo* is a dry riverbed. Such as you might find in a desert where the occasional rain causes the occasional river to flow, leaving a deep, wide groove in the desert floor.

Perdido means "lost" in Spanish. Thus, an *arroyo perdido* is—presumably—an arroyo that cannot be found, whether because it has vanished, or because people have forgotten where it is.

The arroyo that runs through Mickey's neighborhood is not at all lost; it is marked by a dam and a bridge and a big brass plaque. It is also not completely dry; there is almost always a trickle of water at the bottom.

Nonetheless, it is called Arroyo Perdido, and so, consequently, are numerous nearby institutions. For example, Mickey's school, Arroyo Perdido Middle School.

Mickey wishes his school were really *perdido.*

For Mickey, the worst things about school include: class time, which always goes on too long; classmates, all of whom he has known too long; and lunch, which is really much too long when you're sitting alone.

Why alone? Mickey doesn't know.

In years past, he always had a friend or two to eat lunch with, and even to play games with after school. But when he entered middle school, something changed.

Nothing happened per se. People simply stopped talking to him unless he talked to them first, and even then they walked away as soon as they could. It was as though he'd acquired some mysterious condition—visible to everyone but him, and apparently very contagious.

Eventually, Mickey stopped talking to his peers, and started talking to someone who never walks away, and who has the very same condition he has—that is to say, Mickey himself.

No, he doesn't wander around school having full-on conversations with himself. He's not *that* nuts. But he does mumble a bit.

As for lunch, he usually skips it.

Alas, it's much harder to skip P.E.

Uniforms. Locker rooms. Not getting picked for a team. Or worse, getting a pity pick. Mickey hates P.E.

Mickey hates anything to do with sports. Especially team sports.

He particularly dislikes the soccer team, the Teddy Bear Chollas. And the basketball team, the Jumping Chollas.

If you're curious, chollas (pronounced *choyas*) are a type of cactus with deceptively soft- and fuzzy-looking needles. For which reason chollas are sometimes called "teddy bear chollas." These needles have a terrible knack for sticking to whoever passes by. For which reason chollas are sometimes called "jumping chollas."

By the way, the fact that he doesn't like these teams has nothing to do with the fact that his father used to coach the soccer team, or with the fact that his sister plays basketball for her high school.

It doesn't even have to do with the fact that he gets hit by a ball every time he walks by the soccer field or basketball court.

He just doesn't like teams in general.

"GET LOST, SCHOOL!"

"GET LOST, TEDDY BEAR CHOLLAS!"

"GET LOST, JUMPING CHOLLAS!"

8.

Pop!

I know what you're thinking. It seems like Mickey doesn't like anything at all. But that isn't true. There's at least one thing he likes: bubble gum.

Have you ever looked under a desk and wondered who put all that gum there? Well, you don't have to wonder anymore.

It was Mickey. (Mostly.)

blows bubble

POP!

See?

Here's a piece of advice:

Don't chew gum in class.

Here's another piece of advice:

If, against my previous advice, you choose to chew gum in class, don't blow bubbles.

Here's another:

If you simply must blow bubbles, let them gently deflate, don't loudly pop them.

And lastly:

If one loud pop is irresistible, don't repeatedly loudly pop bubbles after your teacher has told you not to. Depending upon your teacher's tolerance level, you may or may not be given another chance to stop popping them.

Mickey's Human Development teacher has a three strikes rule. Or in this case, a three *pops* rule.

Today, after Mickey's third pop, his teacher sends him to the counselor's office.

As it happens, Mickey's teacher *is* the counselor. He is sending Mickey to see himself.

What's more, Mickey's teacher is Mickey's father.

Yes, you read that correctly.

Mickey's teacher = Mickey's counselor = Mickey's father.

When he was promoted from soccer coach to school counselor, Mickey's father inherited the Human Development class.

Do you know what is taught in Human Development? Trust me, it is the last subject you would want your parent to teach.

Mickey has to wait until class is over for his counselor, er, father to arrive.

On the desk is a coffee mug decorated with a dozen or so emojis. At the bottom are the words ***HOW ARE YOU FEELING TODAY?***

Mickey looks from the mug to his reflection in the window. His face doesn't match any of the emojis. Except maybe the one with the straight line for a mouth. Apparently, he is feeling **BLAH**.

Finally, Mickey's father sits down opposite Mickey.

"Why do you test me like that, Mickey?" he asks. "You know I have to treat you just like any other student."

Mickey shrugs.

"Was it the topic of today's class? The Gender Unicorn? I get it—it's embarrassing to hear your dad talk about that stuff. Well, guess what, I don't love it either. But it's my job."

The Gender Unicorn is a chart, in the form of a rainbow-striped unicorn, that teachers use to discuss subjects like gender identity and sexual orientation.

It tends to make students giggle. Or else, as in Mickey's case, blush uncontrollably.

"You told everyone I went through a unicorn phase," Mickey mutters, his face feeling hot all over again. "You know I don't collect them anymore, right?"

"Oh, come on. I was trying to lighten the mood. Consider yourself lucky: If you were homeschooled, I would teach all your classes," his father jokes.

"If I were homeschooled, you wouldn't teach me at all," Mickey responds, not smiling. "Since you don't live at home."

Mickey's father purses his lips. According to the emoji mug, he is feeling **FRUSTRATED**.

"Anyway, I thought we were supposed to be talking about gum," says Mickey.

"Okay." His father takes a breath, forcing himself to calm down. "What message do *you* think you were sending by popping all those bubbles?"

"Uh . . . *pop?*"

"How about *I don't care about this class?* Or *I don't want to be here?* Or maybe *Take a hike, Dad?*"

"No." Mickey hesitates. "Well, not just you. Everyone."

"Everyone?"

"Yeah. And every*thing* . . ." Mickey waves his hand, as if to make the whole room disappear.

His father stares at him. "I have to say, as your counselor, I'm concerned about you, Mickey. Are *you* concerned about you?"

"No. Can I go now?"

Mickey's father drums his fingers on his desk. Mickey stares at the wall.

"All right, here's what you're going to do," his father says after a moment. "You're going to write a list of things you're grateful for."

He walks around his desk and puts a hand on Mickey's shoulder. Mickey shrinks away from him. "If not your family . . . maybe a friend . . . video game . . . favorite cereal . . ." his father continues, backing off. "Anything that makes you go, *Hey, I like that—that's rad!* A rad list."

"*Rad?*" repeats Mickey.

"Yeah, rad. Cool. Awesome. Short for *radical*. Nobody says that anymore?"

"What if I don't think *anything* is rad?"

"Think of it as a thank-you note to the world. A little gratitude to fix that attitude."

Mickey rolls his eyes.

"It's your homework assignment."

"You can't give me homework," Mickey protests. "You're not my teacher. I mean, in here you're not. You're my counselor, like you said."

"Well, a counselor can give you detention. You prefer that? And let me tell you something else, as your father . . ." Mickey's father points at him. "Wipe that gum off your nose."

Mickey glances at his reflection in the window. His face is starting to furrow like the **ANGRY** emoji. He wipes away the furrows along with the gum.

9.

Surprise!

After school, Mickey does not write a thank-you note to the world. Surprise!—he buys more gum.

Down the road from Mickey's school is a small donut shop called Desert Donut where some of the more popular middle school kids hang out after school. Along with a number of high school kids. His sister included. She claims that she is "addicted" to the donut shop's signature coffee drink, the Cactuccino.

Mickey is not a fan of coffee drinks, not even one with green foam and gold sprinkle "needles." Nevertheless, he often goes to Desert Donut because they make a decent plain glazed donut. (Donuts—there's something Mickey likes!) And because they carry Mickey's favorite gum: Bubble Gum King.

Bubble Gum King is an old-fashioned brand that Mickey's mother introduced him to a few years ago.

She loved it when she was young, she said. "There was always this little prize in each pack. Like a puzzle or a set of jacks . . . Have you ever played jacks?"

Mickey was fascinated. He couldn't believe his health-food-loving, sugar-hating mother had ever chewed gum of any kind. It can't even be composted or recycled! He insisted on trying Bubble Gum King immediately.

Bubble Gum King bubble gum is packaged like a deck of cards and features a mustachioed king who resembles the king of hearts on a classic playing card. Unwrapped, the gum is an unpleasant, raw-looking shade of pink. It is so sugary that it has a grainy texture, and it loses its flavor after the first few chews.

Mickey's first reaction was: *Yuck.*

Then he blew a bubble.

With Bubble Gum King bubble gum, he discovered, you can blow bigger, better, balloon-ier bubbles. Bubbles that (usually) only pop when you want them to. Bubbles that have a great deal of what is called tensile strength. (Not to be confused with *tonsil* strength, although arguably you also need tonsil strength to blow bubbles.) When the bubbles pop, they make a loud, satisfying sound. Like the snap of a twig.

One pop and Mickey was hooked.

Today, thankfully, his sister is not hanging out at Desert Donut. There are only a few kids around, and they are absorbed in the shop's single arcade machine, a sit-down driving game called Road Rager. Mickey makes his purchase in peace.

As soon as he walks out, he opens his box of gum, and a slip of waxy paper falls to the ground. Unwilling to bend over, he continues walking. If you don't deliberately toss something, it's not littering, right?

Then he starts to feel the itch of curiosity.

Just like in his mother's time, inside each Bubble Gum King package is a prize. Most often, Mickey throws the prize away, but every once in a while he finds something he wants to keep. Like the little red compass he wears on his keychain. Who knows, maybe the slip of paper is a golden ticket.

He turns around and picks it up.

On one side is a picture of the Bubble Gum King, who seems to be smiling directly at Mickey, as if he has a surprise for him. On the other side is an ad:

DO YOU EVER WISH EVERYONE WOULD GO AWAY?
ARE YOU ANTI-EVERYTHING?
THE ANTI-BOOK IS THE ANSWER!
RETURN THIS COUPON TO CLAIM YOUR PRIZE.

Mickey stares at the paper in his hand. It is waxy and rumpled and looks as though it has been sitting inside the bubble-gum package for years. It does not look as though it was hastily written by his father as a prank. Not that his father has ever been much of a prankster.

In any case, there is no way his father could have gotten to the shop ahead of Mickey, and no way he could have inserted the paper into the package without tearing the wrapper.

It is simply a coincidence that they were only moments ago discussing Mickey's desire to make everyone go away. A bizarre coincidence. A highly unlikely coincidence. But a coincidence nonetheless.

Mickey relaxes—slightly—and reads the ad over again. *Anti-Book?* What's an anti-book?

Mickey knows what *anti* means: It means against or opposed to. As in *antisocial*. (Against the norms of society, or disliking the company of others.) Or *antioxidant*. (Against toxins, like Chewy Charlie's stinky herbal teas.) Or *antidisestablishmentarianism*. (Against . . . well, Mickey doesn't know, but he knows it's one of the longest words in the English language.)

So is an anti-book a book that is against books? Or is it nothing like a book? Is it the opposite of a book? A non-book? An un-book? A de-booked book?

Mickey crumples the coupon and puts it in his pocket.

Car-Boy and Mime-Boy are waiting at their normal spot on the bridge. When Mickey passes them, he tries his best not to walk like a robot. He must be successful, because, instead of imitating Mickey's walk, Mime-Boy pulls out a pink balloon and imitates Mickey's bubble-blowing.

"Ha-ha," says Mickey.

"You know gum is a girl thing, right, ***wipe?" shouts Car-Boy.

"Why, 'cause it's pink?" says Mickey. "That's stupid."

"Think about it, what guys do you know who are always chewing gum?"

"Me."

"Exactly."

Mickey knows it's useless to argue, but he can't help it. "Gum isn't a girl thing or a guy thing."

Car-Boy smiles. "Oh, so it's a *gay* thing. Does your mom always chew gum too?"

Mime-Boy guffaws.

Mickey's face burns. "Gum isn't anything. It's gum!"

"Just calling it like I see it, ****head," says Car-Boy. "Don't be mad."

"I'm not mad!"

Mickey knows what Car-Boy means when he says "Don't be mad." He means *Be mad*. Just like when he says "It's a gay thing," he means *Feel bad*.

Gay is a word Car-Boy says a lot. At least around Mickey. For some reason, he never seems to say it around Mickey's sister. (Or else she seems never to hear.)

Doing homework? "Gay."

The book Mickey's reading? "Gay."

The show Mickey wants to watch? "Gay."

When Mickey drinks the milk left over in his cereal bowl? "Gay."

Mickey wants to tell Car-Boy not to use the word as a dis. "It's not cool," he imagines saying. Or maybe, "Not cool, man. Not cool."

The problem is: He knows what Car-Boy would say back.

Mime-Boy releases the pink balloon. It sails over Mickey's head, spiraling through the air with a high-pitched whine, while the two boys continue to laugh at him.

Mickey doesn't say anything more. He just wishes they would go away. Forever.

As soon as they are out of sight, Mickey takes the ad out of his pocket and reads it again.

DO YOU EVER WISH EVERYONE WOULD GO AWAY?
ARE YOU ANTI-EVERYTHING?

10.

Give me that!

One week later, the Anti-Book appears.

Mickey is lying on the floor of his bedroom, looking up into the middle of a big pink bubble. Not as big as his biggest bubble ever, which was over fourteen inches in diameter and made with five pieces of gum, but big enough to occupy his entire field of vision, if he looks into the bubble's center.

There is a knock on the door. It is his sister's knock. Which is more of a bang than a knock. Alice is not the knocking type. She is the banging type. She is also the barging-in type. That is why his door is locked. And why she has to knock in the first place.

POP!

He peels gum off his face, and addresses the door:

"Get lost."

"With pleasure," Alice chirps from the other side. "I

just thought you might want a package from the king, that's all."

"Ha-ha. Get lost."

"Fine. I'll throw it away . . ."

"Wait!" Mickey smushes his gum into an old math worksheet and springs up. "Don't go! Give me that!"

He throws the door open. She's gone.

"Bring it back!" he shouts, running down the stairs.

He finds his sister in the kitchen, in front of the open fridge. She holds the package high above her head, out of Mickey's reach, while simultaneously lowering a yogurt onto the counter behind her.

"Give it to me. It's mine."

The package is really more of an oversized envelope, with Mickey's name written in neat block letters. *The Bubble Gum King*, it says on the top left corner, with no return address.

"Oh, so now you want it." His sister smiles under her big yellow headphones.

Mickey notices she has dyed her hair bright, fire-engine red. Last time he saw her it was green. Before that, blue.

"What's with you and that gum anyway?" she asks.

"I don't know. Ask your boyfriend. He has theories."

Her eyes narrow. "Why? What did Sean say?"

Sean is Car-Boy's "real" name.

"Nothing."

He said that gum is gay. It sounds so dumb, Mickey hesitates to say it aloud.

"What do you mean nothing?"

She would probably take her boyfriend's side anyway.

"I mean *nothing* nothing," says Mickey. "Just give me the package."

Predictably, she makes him beg. Predictably, she makes him bargain. Predictably, she makes him promise to walk the dog. Morning *and* night. Instead of taking turns.

Mickey hates walking the dog (AKA picking up poop).

"Okay, but only for one day," he stipulates.

"A month."

"Week."

"Deal."

"Nice hair color, by the way," he says, taking his package from her. "But maybe not with the yellow headphones."

"Why not?" Frowning, Alice looks at herself on the screen of her phone.

"I dunno. Kinda mustard and ketchup?"

He relocks his bedroom door before ripping the package open.

11.

Just a book.

There is a slim paperback inside—about the size of a wallet.

The cover is black and white and red, and decorated with one of those spiral patterns that appear to be moving toward you one second and away from you the next. A simple optical illusion you might see on the cover of a book of mazes or party tricks.

THE ANTI-BOOK, it says in big, broken letters, meant to look as though they are exploding.

Near the bottom there is a little crown above a mustache—the Bubble Gum King logo.

Mickey's heart begins to sink. All in all, the Anti-Book looks exactly like what it is: a cheap prize he got for buying a pack of gum.

Quickly, he flips through the pages.

It's just a book. Not even a book. The pages are blank,

making it more of a journal. And not even a very special journal.

It has no lock. No invisible ink pen. No secret codes. No puzzles or tricks. No "I read Anti-Books!" stickers.

Another *anti-* word comes to mind: *anticlimactic*. (It means unexpectedly unexciting, more or less.)

Mickey feels like an idiot. What did he expect?

He remembers hearing about "pet rocks," a gag gift that became inexplicably popular in the 1970s. Pet rocks were just rocks. They didn't even have eyes painted on them.

Maybe this is a pet book.

He opens the Anti-Book again.

Actually, there are five words on the first page. He skipped over them the first time he looked.

To erase it, write it.

Huh?

If you want to erase something, why write it in the first place? Better not to write at all.

Still, Mickey thinks, he ordered the book; he may as well use it.

He decides to write a list of all the things—and people—he would erase from his life if he could. Like the "rad list"—or "thank-you note to the world"—that his father wanted him to write.

Only in reverse. The *anti-* version.

A *bad* list. A *no*-thank-you note to the world.

It will be the opposite of a wish list; it will be an *I-don't-wish-this* list.

When he was younger, Mickey loved practicing calligraphy. He wrote his signature over and over, adding a curl here and a flourish there, until it looked like the signature of a duke or a prince.

Alas, at Mickey's school, it is not considered cool to have fancy or even somewhat neat handwriting. Although—officially—he doesn't care what the other kids think, Mickey has forced himself to adjust. His latest signature is nothing but a scribble.

Tonight, with the rest of his household in bed, and no one looking over his shoulder, he picks up a pencil and writes as he used to write, carefully and ceremoniously, as if he is issuing a royal decree.

Car-Boy
Mime-Boy
Chocolate Chip Charlies
Big Sister
Dog
Mom
Dad

He feels a bit foolish. The list-making is pointless. And yet it is also satisfying. Like looking at your enemies from a distance and squishing them between your fingers.

He continues:

school
Jumping Chollas (aka basketball team, not cactus)
Teddy Bear Chollas (aka volleyball team, not cactus)
cholla chollas (aka actual cactus)
actually ALL cactuses

He keeps at it for hours, pausing only to sharpen his
pencil or rest his hand.

He writes the names of movies that bore him and TV
shows that irritate him. He lists video games that aggra-
vate him and bands that annoy him.

Then he gets started on food and drink and all the
awful things his mother packs in his school lunch.

brown bananas
grainy apples
hummus sandwiches
herbal tea
oat milk
kale (chips, salad, etc.)
kiwi fruit
beets
and did I say beets?
whole wheat pancakes
whole wheat anything

Then comes a long list of random bothersome things.

tight underwear
loose underwear
things that don't come with batteries
impossible-to-open packages
things that break as soon as you buy them
robot arms
the word "gay" (as a dis)

And so on.

Finally, he goes back to people, writing the names of nearly everyone he knows, and of some people he doesn't. When he puts his pencil down, it isn't that he can't think of more people to erase; it's just that he is too tired to keep writing.

He solves the problem in a few words:

everyone else (except me!)

He looks at the clock. It's almost midnight.

Oh no. The dog. He promised to walk the dog.

"Dog!" he shouts. "Come here, Dog!"

When Noodle is not in Mickey's room bothering Mickey, he can most often be found in the family room lounging on the couch. Occasionally, he can even be found in the hallway lying on his own doggy bed.

Tonight, he is in none of those places.

"COME HERE, NOODLE!"

Mickey yells so loudly that he fully expects his sister to yell at him to shut up. Instead, her bedroom door remains closed. She doesn't say anything. Neither does the dog.

Noodle is notoriously lazy, but he can usually be relied upon to respond when he is hungry or when he has to pee.

Probably, Mickey's mother already walked him. Probably, the dog is sleeping in his mother's room. Probably, Mickey can go to bed now and walk Noodle in the morning.

Probably.

12.

Ow!

When Mickey wakes up, the sun is streaming through his bedroom window.

He knows he has overslept even before he looks at the clock. *9:15*. School starts at 8:00. Why didn't his mother wake him? Not that he cares about being late to school. He hates school.

"Ow!"

He hits his head on the edge of the top bunk as he gets out of bed. He hates having a bunk bed. When he was younger his friends would sleep on the top bunk. He would even play up there sometimes when he was alone. These days, he rarely climbs up to the top bunk; he just hits his head on it.

On the way out of his room, he notices the Anti-Book lying open on the floor, next to his now-very-small pencil.

He writes two short words at the bottom of the long list of things he never wants to see again.

bunk bed

By now, Mickey figures, Noodle must be desperate to go outside. But when he calls the dog, the dog doesn't come. Noodle isn't anywhere in the house. Neither is his sister nor his mother nor Chewy Charlie.

Of course, the absence of his fellow humans isn't surprising, given the time.

Probably, his sister is at school. Probably, his mother is taking yoga. Probably, Chewy Charlie is teaching yoga.

They are always doing yoga.

The dog, though—where is the dog?

He glances out the kitchen window, but Noodle isn't in the backyard.

Should he be concerned? Mickey wonders as he drinks the last drop of cereal-flavored milk from his cereal bowl. (Cereal milk—there's something else he likes!)

Once, he and his sister posted Lost Dog flyers all over the neighborhood, only to discover Noodle asleep in a laundry basket.

Just in case, Mickey rifles through the big pile of dirty sheets and towels in the closet next to the washing machine. He finds one of the horns he used to wear on his head in his "unicorn phase" but no dog. He pushes the horn farther into the closet, out of sight.

Briefly, he considers posting Lost Dog flyers again. Then he dismisses the idea. No sense worrying until he knows the dog is really lost.

Probably, his mother has taken Noodle to the vet. Or the groomers. Or something like that.

Probably.

Besides, he is late for school. Not that he cares about being late for school. He hates school. (Did I mention that already?)

As Car-Boy would say, *School is so—*

Mickey searches for the word, but he's forgotten it.

13.

Gone.

It isn't until he goes upstairs to get his backpack that he notices.

There is a wall where his mother hangs all the family holiday and vacation photos. He thought that his mother might take down the pictures of his father when his father moved out, but she didn't.

"We're still very good friends," she reminded Mickey at the time.

"So then we'll have Chrisnukkah together again this year?" Mickey asked skeptically.

"Of course!" said his mother. "The whole point was not to ruin the holidays, remember?"

"The *whole* point?"

"You know what I mean."

Now all the pictures of his father are gone.

In their places: dull scenery photos. And one that is nothing but a blue background.

So much for being good friends, Mickey thinks, marveling at how cleanly his father has been removed from the family gallery. His mother must be a better photo editor than he thought.

But the pictures of his father aren't the only ones that are gone. Also gone: the pictures of his mother and his sister.

They aren't even in the family portraits anymore. Where once his father or mother or sister stood, you can see straight through to the mountain lakes and tropical beaches that serve as backdrops. (Because they live in the desert, most of their family vacations have involved water.)

Only one person remains in any of the pictures:

Mickey.

He stares at the images of his younger self, half expecting to see himself disappear along with the others. But there he remains—in the sand, in the snow, in the ocean—always with that same dumb look on his face, like someone just told a joke that he doesn't get.

Afraid that he is hallucinating, Mickey tears himself away from the wall of photos and runs into his bedroom. Maybe he should lie down for a minute. Maybe he is dreaming and never woke up.

But when he enters his bedroom, he doesn't lie down.

He has no bed to lie on. The bed—upper bunk, lower bunk, the whole thing—is gone.

Where the bed once stood, the floor is now bare, save for a thick layer of dust, a crumpled sock, a pencil, and an open book.

The Anti-Book.

part two:

rad

14.

Poof!

Mickey eyes the Anti-Book for a minute, waiting for something to happen. He still isn't sure whether he is dreaming or going crazy. Either way, it seems like the book should float up into the air or flap its pages like wings or burst into flames or maybe even start talking to him.

But it just lies open on the floor, perfectly ordinary-looking, covered with Mickey's naturally neat and very uncool handwriting.

Is the book safe to touch? He forces himself to pick it up. No flapping. No flames. Not even a spark.

Clutching the Anti-Book, he stumbles downstairs and out the door.

Despite his having grown up in it, Mickey's house has never seemed very special to him. Perhaps that is because it so closely resembles all the other houses in the neighborhood, with their red tile roofs (just like his) and useless tiny balconies (just like his) and cactus gardens that nobody can play in (just like his).

Mickey stands in his driveway, gazing up at his house. It has not changed as far as he can see. And yet something is different. What?

The cactus! That's what's different. Or rather, the *lack* of cactus.

There isn't a single cactus left in the cactus garden. Nor is there a single hole to show that a cactus was once there.

To erase it, write it . . .

He opens the Anti-Book and looks at his list.

"Actually, ALL cactus," he wrote. And—apparently—ALL cactus he erased.

He is dreaming. It's obvious now. Even if it wasn't before.

There is something called lucid dreaming. They discussed it in Human Development. Dreaming when you know you're dreaming.

He is having a lucid dream.

It's weird. But kind of awesome.

Slowly, he spins around.

The rest of the world is just the way he remembers it:

That old pile of dog poop in his front yard. (He accidentally-on-purpose forgot to pick it up two days ago.) His mom's old diesel station wagon, or as he calls it, the "Pee-ew Wagon." (It runs on bio-fuel—i.e., recycled vegetable oil—and always smells slightly rancid.) The two orange cats next door, or as he calls them, the "Copy Cats." (Always moving in tandem, they sneak around the neighborhood, stealing food and wreaking havoc.) And the many noisy tree squirrels, or as he calls them, the "Whirling Squirrelishes." (Always scurrying in different directions, they make it nearly impossible for Mickey to walk the dog.)

As for his neighbors' houses, they're missing their cactus gardens, but otherwise they're clean and tidy as usual. (His house has always looked a little less well-kept than the others.)

He glances at the Anti-Book again. It is just as he thought:

No poop. No Pee-ew Wagon. No Copy Cats. No Whirling Squirrelishes. No neighbors.

His hand shaking slightly, Mickey wrests his pencil from where it is wedged in the middle of the book, and he writes the word as clearly as he can.

poop

Poof!

Before he has even lifted his pencil from the page, the dog poop has vanished. He might as well have waved a magic wand or pushed a delete button.

Pee-ew Wagon

Poof!

Just like that, the station wagon is gone. For a second, Mickey imagines he can still smell the wagon lingering in the air.

The cats narrow their eyes suspiciously.

Copy Cats

Poof!

They disappear without so much as a meow.

Whirling Squirrelishes

Poof!

The trees go quiet.

neighbors

Nothing happens. Mickey realizes his mistake.

neighbors' houses

Poof!

Now his neighbors' houses are gone, leaving nothing in their place except smooth, sandy lots.

He turns and looks at his own house again. There is something irritating about it standing there in its half-erased state when all the others have disappeared without a fuss.

my house

Poof!

Except, in reality, there is no poof. No flash of light. No puff of smoke. His house is just gone.

Completely, inexplicably, magically gone.

Giddy, Mickey runs down the block. Or what a moment ago was his block. Little more than the street and sidewalk remain.

The biggest thing left is Car-Boy's muscle car—the shiny yellow Camaro. Mickey decides to deconstruct the car piece by piece.

the Camaro's windows

Poof! The glass is gone.

Mickey resists the urge to jump into the shiny leather driver's seat. The car must go. Now.

Camaro seats
Camaro dashboard
Camaro steering wheel

Poof! Poof! Poof! The car is an empty shell.

Camaro wheels

Poof! The car falls to the ground with a clang. Gleam-
ing chrome crumples.

Ha! Now *this,* Mickey thinks, is *rad.*

A moment later, he reaches the bridge over the Arroyo
Perdido Dam. Car-Boy and Mime-Boy are nowhere to be
seen, but the mime's black beret is sitting on the ground,
where he sometimes leaves it to collect dollar bills. Perhaps he was mid-performance, opening an invisible door
or walking an imaginary tightrope, when—poof!—he
vanished, leaving only his hat behind.

Mickey picks up the beret and tosses it like a Frisbee
over the side of the bridge. While it's still in the air, he
quickly writes in the Anti-Book.

beret

Poof! The beret disappears mid-flight.

If he wrote the word *bridge,* would he immediately fall
to the dam below? Mickey muses. Or would he be like
one of those old cartoon characters who don't fall until
they notice they're standing on air?

He decides not to test it. Instead, he waits until he gets
to the other side.

bridge

Poof! The bridge is gone. And so is the way home.

Mickey slips the Anti-Book into the pocket of his hoodie and glances around. What next?

The world is his. What's left of it.

15.

Play again?

Desert Donut looks the way it always does. A little dusty around the edges. Littered with coffee cups and cake crumbs. The rows of donuts beckon to Mickey as they always do. It is just that there is nobody to serve them.

He is about to walk behind the glass case and open it for himself when he has a better idea.

glass case

Poof! The donuts fall to the floor, landing in neat rows.

He grabs his usual plain glazed and takes a bite. It's fine. Maybe a tad stale. He is about to take another bite when he reconsiders.

Normally, the fact of it being sugary fried dough would be reason enough to keep eating, but under the circumstances, why not try another donut instead?

He drops the plain glazed onto the floor and chooses a chocolate donut. He takes a bite—pretty good—then drops that one too. He tries a jelly donut. Nice, but not perfect. Then a maple cruller. Better. Then an apple fritter. Even better. Then a blueberry cinnamon roll. Almost worthy of a second bite.

Soon, he has taken a bite out of every donut in the store, as if he is deliberately ruining the entire lot for the next customer. But of course there is no next customer. So . . . no harm done.

Nor are there any kids lined up to play Road Rager. For maybe the first time ever, Mickey is free to sit down at the wheel.

GAME OVER—PLAY AGAIN? flashes on the screen. Someone, it seems, has failed to use all their turns.

About to choose a Jeep, Mickey instead chooses a yellow sports car that looks a lot like the Camaro. Why not smash it up a second time?

He steers wildly, crashing through guard rails and veering far from the race track. Other cars speed past while his goes up in flames.

It seems unfair that he has so much competition.

other cars

Poof!

This time, Mickey lasts much longer and scores much higher.

He raises a fist. Yes! Then, habitually self-conscious, he lowers the fist.

Then he raises it again. After all, no one is watching. He's dreaming. He can jump and shout and dance around the room if he wants to.

He would keep playing, but he has no turns left and no quarters in his pocket. If he wrote *cash register* in the Anti-Book, would coins spill onto the counter?

Never mind. He didn't come here to play Road Rager, or even to eat donuts.

Surprise!—he came for gum.

The candy rack is on the opposite side of the room from Road Rager, to the left of the cash register. He stares at the rack in consternation. The box with the Bubble Gum King logo on it is empty. At the very moment that he has unlimited access!

If only he could write the word *gum* in the Anti-Book and make a pack of bubble gum fall from the sky, he thinks as he walks out the door. Too bad the Anti-Book only makes things disappear.

Automatically, Mickey heads in the direction of school.

He wants to make sure his school is really gone. He wants to stand where it once stood and say "Bye-bye" or "Ha-ha" or "Nyah-nyah." Or maybe he just wants, for once, not to be called upon to say anything at all.

Although the day is warm and sunny, Mickey shivers. He has the odd sensation that he's being followed. Or odder still, that he's following someone else.

He spins around, and for a half second he thinks he sees a boy, or rather, the shadow of a boy. Then he realizes the shadow is his own.

Relax, he tells himself. It was just the breeze on your neck.

He quickens his stride.

At first, he isn't certain he has reached his destination. The new view of the mountains confuses him. But he soon confirms he is standing in his school parking lot. Or what was once his school parking lot. He can tell by the bus stop and broken bench in front.

The school is most definitely gone. Not just the buildings, but also the bike racks and school buses, the chalkboards and tablets, the lunch trays and lockers. He doesn't even spy a crumpled homework assignment.

Everything has vanished.

Correction: almost everything.

One thing, for some reason, has escaped the Anti-Book: the big, illuminated, marquee-style sign that stood next to the school's front steps.

The sign is dark now, but Mickey can still read the words:

WELCOME TO ARROYO
PERDIDO MIDDLE SCHOOL
HOME OF THE CHOLLAS

He might be looking into the past, when the school was an idea not yet built. Or far into the future, when the school is a distant memory.

Either way, this dream is a trip.

16.

Bzzzzz.

His reverie is interrupted by a fly.

Bzzzzz.

A loud, annoying housefly buzzing in his ear.

fly

He writes the word reflexively, almost without think-ing. Then he adds *house* in front of it—housefly—just to be sure he is specifying the right fly.

There are, after all, many kinds of flies, including all the fruit flies that live in his kitchen, feasting on Chewy Charlie's leftover cookie dough. And then there are the fly-things that aren't flies at all. Dragonflies or flying fish, for example.

Poof!

Bye, fly.

"Phew!" says Mickey aloud.

Peace and quiet are his once more.

But still he feels uneasy.

Where did that fly go? he wonders. Did he erase it permanently or temporarily? Is it gone forever or just for now?

If he's really lucid dreaming, he should be able to make it come back somehow.

He opens the Anti-Book and reads the inscription again.

To erase it, write it.

Perhaps the reverse is true, as well, he thinks.

To write it—or in this case, to *rewrite* it—erase it.

In other words, to bring a thing back, erase the word that made the thing disappear. It makes sense. In a way.

He will perform an experiment.

Of course, he doesn't want his whole world back. Not yet. He's only just begun to enjoy his newfound solitude. He simply wants to know that the world will return when he needs it to.

Using the end of his pencil he erases the last word he wrote: *housefly.*

He waits a moment. He hears no buzzing. He sees no insect anywhere.

He glances down at the Anti-Book. A faint trace of the word lingers on the page—so faint you wouldn't be able to read it if you didn't already know what it said. Still, a trace is a trace.

He erases the word all over again, pushing down so hard that the page almost tears.

He waits another moment or two. Or three. Or four.

The fly does not come back.

Mickey looks around at the empty school parking lot. A terrible feeling starts to form somewhere in the pit of his stomach.

What if this isn't a dream after all?

What if it's not reversible? This thing he's done to the world. This way he's *un*done the world.

What if his school is gone for good? And not just the school, but the students . . . the teachers . . . his father . . . his mother . . . sister . . . dog . . .

Don't panic, he tells himself. Just think.

Why didn't the fly come back?

Maybe because *housefly* is the last word he wrote in the Anti-Book. Maybe the fly won't return until all the other things he listed return as well.

Sitting on the ground, he flips back to the very beginning of his very long list.

He erases the first word: Car-Boy.

Nothing happens.

Next: Mime-Boy.

He erases it. Nothing happens.

Chocolate Chip Charlies

Big Sister

Dog

He keeps going and going, furiously erasing words

until his fingers are sore and covered in pencil lead, and his pencil's eraser is long past useful.

And *still* nothing happens.

Apparently, the Anti-Book works in one direction only. It destroys, but never creates.

Mickey shoves the Anti-Book into his pocket and staggers to his feet. The terrible feeling in his stomach has risen into his throat like bile. He wants to throw up.

What now?

Probably, his logic is faulty. If he isn't wrong about the Anti-Book, then he's wrong about lucid dreams. Just because he can't control the world around him—it doesn't mean that he's not dreaming.

Somewhere, somehow, the world is just as he left it. And everyone he knows is fine.

The alternative is intolerable. Unthinkable. Unimaginable.

Then don't imagine it, he tells himself. Keep going.

Something dark and fast flickers across the edge of Mickey's vision.

He was right—he *is* being followed!

Or maybe he's just antsy. When he looks around for his pursuer, he sees no one.

Instead, his eyes lock on the school's old welcome sign.

The sign is lit up with words again, but the words have changed. Indeed, there is no longer any mention of the school at all.

WELCOME TO
THE ANTI-WORLD
HOME OF THE
BUBBLE GUM KING

Anti-World? As in Anti-Book?

And it's the home of the Bubble Gum King?

Does that mean the king is an actual, living, breathing person? The idea excites and disturbs Mickey at the same time.

Pop stars, YouTubers, celebrity chefs—you assume they exist even if your paths are not likely to cross. The Bubble Gum King is more like a character out of a cartoon. A mascot, not a man.

And yet in some weird way, for the past six months or so, he has almost seemed more real to Mickey than the real people in his life. More than once Mickey has held a pack of gum in his hand, and stared at the king's picture, wishing himself out of his own world and into the king's.

And now . . .

Of course, realistically, *Home of the Bubble Gum King* could mean anything. Maybe the Anti-World is a fast-food restaurant, and the king is nothing more than a mustache and crown rotating on a pillar.

Mickey glances over his shoulder, and sees nothing except for an empty parking lot and . . .

. . . the Anti-World sign?

The sign has moved 180 degrees. Instantly. By itself.

He looks forward again. And there's the sign again, in its original location.

Whichever way he turns, the sign is right in front of him. It is like being in a hall of mirrors. Except without the hall and without the mirrors.

Experimentally, he steps toward the sign; it looks more or less normal. He touches one of the poles that the sign stands on; it *feels* more or less normal too.

And yet, when he tries to walk around it, the sign moves, always staying slightly ahead of him, as if playing a game. A very frustrating game.

To keep it in place, he tries holding on to the sign while he walks. It remains stationary for one tantalizing moment, only to whip around, making Mickey feel as though he is spinning.

The sensation reminds him of being swung in circles by his father when he was little. "Dizzy yet? Dizzy yet?" his father would ask. "Not yet! Not yet!" Mickey would say, wanting the feeling to last forever.

It strikes Mickey now that his father must have been very dizzy himself. And yet to make Mickey happy his father kept spinning—until finally they would fall to the ground, laughing and laughing.

When was the last time they laughed together?

Mickey drops his hand.

He doesn't want to think about his father. He doesn't want to think about his family.

Before Mickey can plan his next move he hears a familiar sound.

Bzzzzzzzz.

The sound is faint but insistent.

Bzzzzzzzz.

It is, unmistakably, a fly. But is it the old fly or a new fly? How can one tell?

The buzzing seems to be coming from somewhere above his head.

Looking up, Mickey is momentarily blinded by the sun. As his eyes adjust, he makes a surprised, burping, slurping sound that would be very embarrassing in other circumstances.

High in the sky, at a midpoint between a small puffy cloud and a long fading jet stream, there is a tiny dot. A tiny dot that is growing less tiny by the second.

Something is falling. But what?

As it comes closer, the dot's shape becomes clearer. It's not round; it's square. In fact, it's not a dot at all.

It's a house.

Heart racing, Mickey takes a step backward. He

doesn't want to be squashed like a certain old witch in a certain old story.

Then, quite suddenly and unexpectedly, the house stops falling.

And hovers right in front of his nose.

17.

Hi!

The reason the house looked as though it were falling from such a great height is that it is so little. It is not much bigger than a Monopoly house. But rather than being made of green plastic, it has a red tile roof and two multi-paned windows that resemble nothing so much as a pair of bulging, insectoid eyes.

On either side of the house: a veiny, translucent wing.

Mickey stares in wonder. Seeing a house disappear is one thing; seeing a house fly is another.

Bzzzzz, says the flying house.

Or so Mickey first hears it. It takes him a second to realize that what he's actually hearing—spoken in a tiny, buzzy voice—is the word *hi*.

"Hi?" echoes Mickey.

"Yes, hi. It is short for hello," comes the slightly impa-tient response. "Would you prefer I were more formal? Or do you not speak English? Parlez-vous français? Hablas español? Sprichst du Deutsch?"

In his mind, Mickey sees the Anti-Book open in front of him. *Housefly*, he wrote—and then erased. And now, a housefly, of a sort, has returned. "Well? Speak up, dear."

As the tiny house flies closer and closer, Mickey has an intense desire to scratch his nose, but he refrains. He has the distinct feeling that this flying house wouldn't consider it polite.

"N-no, I speak English. And, um, hi is fine," he stammers. "So you're a . . . housefly?"

"Excuse me? Do I look like a housefly? Is my body black and fuzzy and divided into sections? No, you've got it backward. I am a *flyhouse*!"

"Oh, sorry!" says Mickey, struggling to keep up with this strange and sensitive creature.

So the housefly has become a flyhouse.

Perhaps the Anti-Book *is* reversible, but only in reverse: Sure, you can bring things back . . . if you don't mind them coming back backward.

"What's your name?" he asks.

"A name! What a lovely idea!" exclaims the flyhouse. "Might I have a moment to ponder? What do you think of *Felicity*? Meaning happiness . . . rightness . . . contentment. *Felicity the Flyhouse*. It suits me, does it not?"

"Sure, it suits you," says Mickey cautiously.

"Then Felicity it is!" the flyhouse buzzes with satisfaction. "Now that that's settled, I have a request: May I have your poo?"

"What?"

"Your poo, dear. Your fecal matter. It's somewhere on you—the seat of your pants perhaps?" Felicity flies in circles around Mickey, inspecting him inch by inch. "Not a single one of my eyes can see it, but I can smell it. And it smells absolutely divine!"

"But I don't have any poo."

"Come on. Don't be shy. I know what I'm smelling. I wasn't born yesterday—I was born two minutes ago! Teehee! But seriously, where is it?"

"I swear!"

"My, my, you are a delicate one, aren't you? Ashamed of a little poo." She lingers by his nose again. "I have this funny desire to take you inside and shelter you under my roof. You could have the bedroom behind my third eye down from the left. Would you like that?"

Mickey stares at the associated windowpane. "I think that's where my bedroom is . . . was."

"Wonderful! Well, it's all yours."

"I don't think I'd fit."

Could it really be his house, shrunken many times over, hovering in front of him? It sure looks like his house. Well, his house with wings. And better manners.

Felicity sighs dramatically. "Details! Details! . . . Now back to that intoxicating smell. Did you fart? Is that it?"

"No."

"Tell the truth."

"I am!"

"So you're saying this poo I'm smelling—it has nothing to do with you. It's not on you. It's not in you. It does not come from you—in either solid or gaseous form."

"No. I mean, right. It's not mine."

"Let me look into your eyes. They say that eyes are the window to the soul, but your eyes don't look anything like windows! Mine, however . . ."

The flyhouse blinks her windowpanes in a self-satisfied sort of way, then peers deeper into Mickey's eyes. They start to cross.

"Hm. Only two eyes and you can't even keep them straight. And yet, believe it or not, I believe you!"

Felicity stops inspecting Mickey and starts inspecting the gravel at his feet. "That poo has got to be somewhere around here."

Mickey sniffs. "Actually, I kind of smell it too. I think it's dog poop."

In fact, it smells like his own dog's poop. Then again, to Mickey, dog poop is dog poop. He's not a connoisseur.

"Ah! Dog. I should have known." Felicity flies in increasingly larger circles. "Where art thou, mine poo? You can't hide forever . . ."

Suddenly, she stops circling. "Now, fancy that!"

"What is it?"

"What indeed!" Beneath Felicity, a glittering gold lump sits in a patch of grass. "Golden poo! Have you ever heard of such a thing? I haven't. Of course, I'm only two minutes old. Well, three now. My, how time flies when you're . . . flying."

Mickey shakes his head. The gold poop really is quite remarkable. Almost . . . beautiful.

As he examines it, he remembers that he put poop in the Anti-Book. The *word poop,* that is.

Backward or forward, *poop* is *poop.* (It's a palindrome.) Thus, if it's true that things written in the Anti-Book come back backward, the old poop and the new poop should be the same poop.

Why gold, then? Maybe because gold is the opposite of poop? Something you would never flush down a toilet?

Felicity scoops golden bites into her open-door mouth. "Yum! Gold or not, this poop is delicious. Rich. Unctuous. Earthy. But with a grassy finish. Glorious! Would you like some?"

Felicity rises in the air, carrying a tiny, shiny chunk of golden poop for Mickey to taste.

"No. I'm good, thanks."

"You're sure? A growing boy like you?"

Mickey's eyes land on the Anti-World sign, which is definitely not standing where he last saw it. "So, do you know where we are? I mean, what is the Anti-World?"

"Goodness! Don't they teach you anything in school?"

Felicity lets out a merry laugh, bobbing in the air. "The Anti-World is the world that exists after you make the real world disappear, naturally."

"So none of this is real?" asks Mickey, unsure what answer he wants to hear.

"Ah, now that's a question for philosophers, not fly-houses."

"Well, do you know how to get back to the real world at least?"

"Me? I only just landed in this one . . . Wait, what's that?" Felicity asks, freezing mid-flight. "Uh-oh. I think somebody has come to steal my breakfast!"

"I seriously doubt that," says Mickey, looking around. He doesn't see anyone.

"You'd be surprised," says Felicity. "When it comes to poo, some folks have no scruples whatsoever. And with this gorgeous golden nugget, all bets are off."

Buzzing like an angry hornet, she flies low over the ground, carrying a little lump of gold poop between her legs, ready to fight anyone who dares look at it.

Like a mother with a baby, Mickey thinks.

Not that his own mother has ever been especially protective. She's one of those parents who believes in the "importance of taking risks."

When he was younger, she used to inspect his legs, hoping to see skinned knees. "Go! Run wild!" she would say. "You can't learn from your mistakes if you don't make any."

If only she could see him now. He's definitely making some mistakes. Big ones.

Mickey watches Felicity pass straight under the Anti-World sign, as if it were a perfectly normal, stationary object.

Should he follow? No doubt his mother would tell him to.

As a test, he sticks his hand between the two poles supporting the sign. Sure enough, his hand gets through. The sign doesn't move.

And that's when Mickey hears the tiny frightened shrieks coming from the other side.

18.

Aaaaaaaaaaayyyyy!!!

"Aaaaaaaaaaayyyyy!!!"

"Mickey, come here quick!" he hears Felicity shout.

Without hesitating any further, he darts underneath the sign . . . and finds himself standing on a gravel parking lot very much like the one he was standing on a second ago.

If the sign is a portal to another world, this new world is not dramatically different from the old. They could be mirror images of each other.

"Aaaaaaaaaaayyyyy!!!"

The flyhouse hovers two inches above the ground.

"I think it's a human!" she says, as if she has discovered a new exotic species.

The shrieks redouble in volume.

"Aaaaaaaaaaayyyy!!! Aaaaaaaaaaayyyyyyyyyy!!!"

Mickey crouches down as low as he can. He doesn't see the source of the shrieks until he's right above it.

Felicity was right: It *is* a human. A human girl. A very small human girl. No more than three inches tall. Not quite as strange as a flying house, perhaps, but almost.

She is cowering behind a rock, and covering her head with her hands.

"Uh . . . Uh . . ." Mickey stammers, eyes agog.

What do you say to such a tiny person? Should he acknowledge their size difference or ignore it?

He finally settles on: "Hi. Are you okay?"

If she replies, he doesn't hear.

Awkwardly, he scoops her up to have a better look.

"Aaaaaaaaaaaaaaaaaaayyyyyyyyyyyyyyyyyyyyyy!!!!!!!!!"

"Is that a *yes*?"

She pounds on his thumb with her fists. "Put me down!"

"Ow! Okay, okay. Sorry." Mickey drops her on the ground.

"Touch me again and you'll really be sorry!"

The little girl stares defiantly at Mickey. He stares back at her. The yellow headphones look familiar. So does the red hair.

Could it be . . . ?

"ALICE?!?"

"MICKEY!?!"

Felicity buzzes curiously. "Who is it?"

"My big sister," says Mickey. "I think."

Felicity chortles. "She doesn't look very big."

The flyhouse swoops down for a closer look.

"Aaaaaaaaayyyyyyyy!" Mickey's now-little big sister shrieks again.

"Relax, dear, I'm not going to hurt you," says Felicity. "You'd think the poor girl had never seen a house before!"

"Well, not a talking, flying one, no, I haven't," says Alice, backing up against another rock.

"Her name is Felicity," Mickey says as he pushes himself to his feet and brushes himself off.

He's not sure how to feel about Alice's reappearance: relieved that she is alive, or distressed that she is only the size of his finger.

Alice stares up at him. "Mickey, you're giant! Or am I just having a nightmare?"

"I don't know. If you are, I'm having the same one."

Is that possible, he wonders, to share a dream?

"Seriously," Alice insists, "what is going on?"

"Seriously? I didn't get big. You got small." To demonstrate, Mickey brings his hands together until there is an Alice-size gap between them.

"No, seriously!"

"Seriously! You're my little sister now. My little big sister."

He doesn't say anything about the Anti-Book, or about how he wrote the words *big sister* and made her disappear, or about how he erased those words only to see her reappear in this smaller, opposite form.

"Seriously? I'm little? Like *little* little?"

"Yes. *Seriously* seriously. Look around."

"At what? Last thing I remember, I'm lying in bed, texting my boyfriend and avoiding my Algebra II homework.

Then I wake up and there's no bed. Just a bunch of boulders. And a giant version of my little brother staring into my face."

"Those aren't boulders, they're pebbles . . . gravel. You're in a parking lot."

"I am?"

Mickey points. "See that? That's a bottle cap. And that's a penny. And that's a candy bar wrapper."

"Oh my gosh, you're right!" Amazed, she inspects the wrapper. It's big enough to wrap *herself* in. "What happened to me? How do I change back?"

"How should I know?"

His face reddening, Mickey glances down at the Anti-Book. Only a small corner of the book is visible peeking out of his sweatshirt pocket. He leaves it where it is.

"Where are Mom and Dad? Are they still normal or did everyone turn little except you?"

"I don't know," says Mickey quickly. "I haven't seen them."

It's not a lie exactly. Anyway, there's no reason to tell her about the Anti-Book. She would never let him hear the end of it. And what good would it do? The Anti-Book includes no instructions for restoring sisters to their normal size.

Alice looks at her phone, which has shrunk along with her. "My phone's not working—no bars. What about Sean?"

"Car-Boy? No idea." But I hope *he's* little too, Mickey thinks ungenerously.

"We have to find him. And our parents," Alice declares, furiously texting on her tiny cell phone even though she's not getting service. "Somebody must know why I'm the size of a tube of lip balm."

"How are we supposed to find them?" asks Mickey.

"We can start by going home."

"But . . . w-we can't get home anymore," he stammers.

"What do you mean?"

"Yes, what do you mean?" asks Felicity. "Surely there is some way home? Did you not buy a round-trip ticket?"

His little big sister is staring up at him, waiting.

"Well, for one thing, the bridge is gone."

"Gone?" Alice repeats.

Mickey nods. He can't bring himself to say that their house is gone too.

Not *really* gone, he assures himself. Not *gone* gone.

He just has to figure out how to get back to it. Or to get their house back from wherever it went.

The Anti-Book is the key. But he's already erased everything he wrote in it. What else can he do? How does he rewrite the world into existence?

"Was there an earthquake?" asks Alice. "A tornado?"

He shakes his head.

"Alien attack? Zombie apocalypse?"

He shakes his head again.

"Don't you have any idea what happened?"

Mickey squirms. "Nope. Everything just disappeared."

Alice slumps down onto a pebble. A tear rolls down her cheek.

Mickey looks at her aghast. His sister almost never

cries. The last time was when their parents announced their separation.

The time before that was when Mickey was three. Alice built a tower of lawn furniture on the back patio. She shoved Mickey's old rocking chair on top, and told him to rock.

"Pretend it's a unicorn . . . No, not like that!" she yelled, too late. "Unicorns don't have wings!!!"

The patio was concrete. He needed twelve stitches.

She cried on and off for days.

Felicity buzzes around Alice. "Now, now, dear, it can't be that bad."

Mickey is trying to think of something sympathetic to say—*You're still my best big sister even though you're little?*—when she pulls herself together.

"What about our dog?" Alice asks, wiping away her tears. "Have you seen Noodle anywhere?"

Mickey shakes his head.

"He always knows how to get home."

Alice uses the boulder (or pebble) she's been leaning against to prop herself up.

She glances around. "Maybe if we find him, he can lead us there. Or at least help us find our parents. He'll sniff them out or something."

"Our parents broke up, remember?" says Mickey.

"So? They're still our parents. And they still have smells!"

"Canines are known for their finely tuned sense of smell," agrees Felicity.

"Have you tried calling him?" asks Alice.

Mickey looks at the phone in Alice's hand. "On the phone? He's a dog."

"Is this all just a joke to you?"

"No. Sorry."

"Then call him already," says Alice. "Maybe he's closer than you think."

"Fine." Mickey cups his hands around his mouth, and walks in circles, yelling as loud as he can. "NOOOODLE! NOOOOODLE! NOOOOOOOODLE!"

There are no answering barks.

He yells the dog's name several more times, his face turning red with exertion.

Still no answer.

To Mickey's surprise, he realizes that he is disappointed. Is it possible that he misses his dog? The dog he has told to get lost more times than he can count?

Mulling over this strange new feeling, Mickey sees a movement in the corner of his eye. Noodle? He turns—

It's his follower again!

This time, Mickey is certain that he isn't looking at his shadow, because he is looking toward the sun. And in front of the sun is a boy. Or maybe the hologram of a boy. Mickey can see right through him.

In a blink, the boy is gone.

"Hey, did you guys see that?" he asks. "There was someone standing there a second ago."

"All I can see from here is your shoe," says Alice. "By the way, your laces are untied."

"I didn't see anyone, but that doesn't mean much," says Felicity. "I'm afraid my eyesight, while wonderfully multi-faceted, is quite poor."

As the flyhouse flutters nervously in the breeze, a piece of paper blows right past her. It lands in front of Alice.

It's a flyer from someplace called Bubble Mountain and it's pink. Bubble-gum pink.

Mickey is about to kick it away when he notices a familiar crown and mustache logo.

As he picks up the flyer, his heart thrums with excitement.

For the moment, he forgets about his dog. He forgets about the holographic boy. He even forgets about getting his sister home.

19.

The king rules!

Mickey holds the flyer tight, as though afraid it might blow away.

***BUBBLE-BLOWING CONTEST ***
AT BUBBLE MOUNTAIN

GRAND PRIZE:
A LIFETIME'S SUPPLY OF BUBBLE GUM

WINNER WILL BE CROWNED
BUBBLE GUM PRINCE OR PRINCESS
HEIR TO THE ANTI-THRONE

BY ORDER OF HIS MAJESTY
THE BUBBLE GUM KING

Directions on back

So there really is a Bubble Gum King! And the winner of his contest will be his heir!

If ever a contest was made for Mickey, it is this one.

His hand trembling slightly, he turns over the paper.
On the back is a map that looks more like a
maze—a strange, spiraling maze with
Bubble Mountain in the center.

GO MAD. TAKE A WRONG TURN. MAKE A BAD CHOICE. AND YOU'LL BE RIGHT THERE!

Mickey's heart sinks. Such ridiculous directions—they couldn't be real.

"Bubble Mountain?!" cries his sister, looking up at the flyer. "Nope. No way. We're going home."

"Yes, home, please," says Felicity, who has been hovering close by. "I may not have long to live, and I want to see you tucked safely into your own beds before I die."

"Why, are you sick?" asks Alice, looking at the flyhouse with concern.

"No. It's just that flies only live a week or two at most . . . If only I could make room for you under my roof! I'm just a Musca domestica at heart."

Mickey is struggling to come up with a response when he hears a voice coming from over his shoulder.

"Tell them Bubble Mountain *is* the way home."

It's the see-through boy again—now lying on the bus stop bench with his feet up, completely at ease.

He is still mostly invisible, but from what Mickey can see, he looks like he's about Mickey's age.

He sits up and grins at Mickey. "S'up, bro."

Mickey stares at him. "Who are you? You've been following me."

"Me? I'm not exactly the follower type," he says, not exactly denying it. "You know who's got followers? And a ton of likes? The king. He's, like, the original influencer. What!!!" The see-through boy laughs.

"So you're saying there really is a Bubble Mountain?" asks Mickey cautiously. "The Bubble Gum King really exists?"

"Sure he does. The king rules! Get it? He's the ruler of the Anti-World. He makes the rules. But also, like, *he rules* . . . What!!!" The boy laughs again. He cracks himself up.

Mickey smiles nervously, uncertain how to react. The invisible boy is one of those outgoing, jokey kids who make him feel awkward and self-conscious. At the same time, he has a vaguely familiar quality, as if they'd been friends in preschool.

Not that Mickey can remember ever having an invisible friend. Not even an imaginary one.

"Anyway, he's the guy who can tell you the rules of the Anti-Book. He knows everything about the Anti-World. He can get your sister home."

"You know about the Anti-Book?" Mickey sputters.

"Duh."

The boy nods at the book, which is still sticking out of the left-hand pocket of Mickey's hoodie.

Instinctively, Mickey covers it with his hand. He doesn't want Alice to see it. Or the boy to see it, for that matter.

"And if you win the contest, you'll have gum coming out of your ears." The boy's eyes twinkle mischievously. "I mean, *if* you like gum . . ."

He's teasing. He knows I like gum, thinks Mickey, thoroughly unnerved. How does he know I like gum?

Alice looks askance at her brother. "Who are you talking to?"

The boy shakes his head. Better not tell her.

"Some guy," says Mickey, ignoring him. "He just kinda showed up."

"What guy?"

"Uh, right there." Mickey indicates the bench. The boy listens with an amused expression on his face. "He's sort of hard to see."

"Are you messing with me? Because I don't have much of a sense of humor right now."

His sister appears completely serious. Evidently, she can't see the boy at all.

"This really isn't the time for jokes," Felicity concurs. Evidently, she can't see the boy either.

"You're right. I was talking to myself," says Mickey. It seems easier not to argue.

The boy smirks. Told you!

"It's just . . . I was excited 'cause I figured out how to get home," Mickey announces, trying to sound upbeat. "And how to make you big again and everything," he adds optimistically.

"Really?" Alice offers a tentative smile.

He holds up the map. "We're going to see the king!"

Her smile fades. "You and that bubble gum. You just want to enter that contest."

"No. Well, yeah, kinda," admits Mickey. (With his sister, there's no use pretending.) "But think about it . . ."

He repeats what the boy said about the king, minus any reference to the Anti-Book.

The tiny girl regards her brother with a not-so-tiny dose of skepticism. "What makes you think he's a person and not just a brand like Burger King or Bubble Yum or whatever?"

Mickey glances at his invisible companion. The boy shrugs unhelpfully.

"I just do, okay?" says Mickey.

Alice sighs. "I guess it can't hurt to try."

The see-through boy grins and gives Mickey a thumbs-up.

Mickey feels like he has achieved a victory, but he can't tell whose: his or the boy's.

"All right, so let's go, then—" he says, reaching for his sister.

"Wait!" says Alice. "You don't pick someone up without asking for their consent. Haven't I taught you anything?"

"Sorry. If you want to walk, walk."

She looks around. Compared to her the parking lot is as vast as an ocean. "Okay. But gently! You know I get carsick. I might get . . . hand-sick."

Mickey opens his hand in front of her, allowing her to walk into his palm of her own volition. "How can you still be so bossy? When you're so little."

She climbs up his arm to just below his shoulder, then grabs the edge of his hood to pull herself the rest of the way up.

"I'm not bossy. I'm assertive."

He looks down his nose at her. It's like having a mouse on his shoulder. "Fine. How can you still be so assertive when you're so little?"

"Gah. Your breath!" Alice exclaims. "Did you even brush your teeth this morning?"

"You really want me to answer that?"

"No. Just don't breathe on me." She buries her face in his sweatshirt.

"So how do we get there?" Mickey whispers over Alice's head.

The see-through boy opens his hands and shakes his head, as though the answer should be obvious. "Didn't you read the directions? *GO MAD*, dude."

Unlike Mickey, he speaks at full volume. But Alice doesn't react. Neither does Felicity.

Evidently, they can't hear him any better than they can see him.

"Go mad like go crazy?" asks Mickey.

"Sorta? See, the Anti-World is divided into states."

"Like the United States?"

"More like states of mind. Emotions? Feelings?" The boy makes a face. "Yuck, right?"

Chuckling, he gets off the bench and points to the map in Mickey's hand.

"See that? The biggest one is Mad. Then there's Bad, Sad, and somewhere far, far away, Glad. I've never been to Glad, but whatever, it sounds totally boring anyways."

"And Bubble Mountain is in Bad?" Mickey guesses, studying the map.

"Yup. Bad is rad! You go there, you don't ever want to leave. It's like, ding ding ding! You won! What!!!"

Mickey smiles to himself. No doubt, his father would feel vindicated hearing such a cool young guy use the word *rad*.

"The only problem with Bad is that to get there you gotta go through Mad."

"What's wrong with that?" asks Mickey.

"Nothing. As long as you stay chill."

The boy glances at his bare wrist as if he's wearing a watch. "Sorry, man, time to bounce. Hard for me to stick around too long in this condition . . . See ya—wouldn't wanna be ya!" he shouts—and instantly vanishes.

Mickey bites his lip in frustration.

Alice sits up straight on her brother's shoulder. "Is the Anti-World getting to you or something? Because, as your sister, I have to tell you, you sound insane talking to yourself like that."

"Yeah, you could say it's getting to me," says Mickey, returning to the map. It gets more and more confusing the closer he looks at it.

Felicity flies down to Mickey's eye level. "To Bubble Mountain, then?"

"Yeah, but we have to 'go mad' first," says Mickey. "Or go *to* Mad, I guess. And from the map it looks like . . ."

He takes a few steps forward, looking from the map to his surroundings.

"Wait, where did it go?"

He spins around, remembering the Anti-World sign's tendency to move.

"Whoa!" Alice clings to his sweatshirt hood, the motion throwing her first one direction, then the opposite. "Maybe not hand-sick, but definitely shoulder-sick!"

"The sign," says Mickey, oblivious to his sister's plight. "It's gone."

Last time he looked, it was everywhere. Now, it's nowhere.

20.

Jump! Jump! Jump!

Mickey's sister looks sideways at him. "You need a sign to tell you you're in the school parking lot?"

"Not usually."

"How about unusually? Like, now?"

As if sensing trouble, she rolls down his sleeve and lands smack in the palm of her big little brother's hand.

Alice has always been good at sensing trouble, Mickey reminds himself. When she isn't making it.

"I told you," he says. "Things aren't the same. Look— my school is gone. And we're not even on gravel anymore. Or, wait—"

A white line on the ground has caught Mickey's eye.

He brushes sand away with his foot, and sees that the line continues for at least several yards. Next to it, there are big letters—or the traces of big letters—on the ground.

GO CH L S! G H LLAS!

"I think we just walked over to the soccer field," he says.

"The soccer field?" Alice repeats. "Are you sure? It looks like it hasn't been used in a hundred years."

Mickey scratches his head. It's true, the ground is covered with sand and rock and cactuses.

An ancient soccer field. Is that a thing?

Tentatively, he walks deeper into the soccer field/desert. They are surrounded by more and more cactuses.

"Do those cactuses look like big hands to you?" he asks uneasily.

"*Cacti* not *cactuses*," says his sister.

"Actually, both are correct," says the flyhouse. "In fact, the word *cactus* itself can be a plural noun. Like fish."

"What were you—a schoolhouse in another life?" grumbles Alice, clearly annoyed at having her correction corrected. "Anyway, they're saguaros, not some random cactus. But I see what you mean about hands, Mickey. Look, that one's making a fist!"

"Uh-huh," says Mickey. "And that one's making a peace sign."

"Not anymore." Alice leans out of Mickey's hand. "Now it's . . . flipping us off?!"

Mickey opens his mouth in surprise. There is no doubt about it: The saguaro is giving them the finger.

"Sheesh," he says. "What did we ever do to it?"

"I'm just glad it's stuck in the ground," says his sister.

Before Mickey can respond, the saguaro that looks like a fist rearranges its "fingers" and points at him.

He flinches. The teeny sibling in his palm shrieks.

"Why is it pointing at us!?"

Felicity freezes midflight. "Shh. Do you hear that?"

"What?" asks Mickey.

His sister grips his thumb. Tense.

"Kids, I think," says the flyhouse. "Are there many out in the wild?"

And then Mickey hears it too: Whoops. And hollers. And shouts of rage.

And a few unrepeatable insults.

"Such language!" exclaims Felicity. "Are they talking to *us*?"

"I hope not," says Mickey. "I hate kids."

Alice gives her brother a look.

"What?" he says. "Aren't you always telling me you're not a kid anymore?"

And suddenly they're surrounded.

But not by kids.

Short furry-looking cactuses—chollas—are dropping into the field from all sides.

On their left, chollas jump up and down in a fury.

"JUMP! JUMP! JUMP! ON YOUR TEAM WE DUMP!"

The chollas are a jumble of branches that break and re-form with every leap. Bits and pieces fly in all directions.

"The Jumping Chollas!" Mickey exclaims, astonished.

On the right, a second group of chollas are growling in anger.

"HUG! HUG! HUG! SQUEEZE UNTIL THEY WHEEZE!"

They wobble toward the Jumping Chollas with their needle-covered arms wide open.

"And those are the Teddy Bear Chollas," Mickey adds unnecessarily.

"They do look rather soft and cuddly," says Felicity, rising slightly higher in the air, above the fray.

"Trust me, they're not," says Mickey, thinking about what he wrote in the Anti-Book. Is it because he specified that he meant the Cholla teams and *not* the cholla cactus that the teams have *become* cactus?

The flyhouse looks dubiously at the chollas. "It's hard to believe those unruly cacti have the discipline to play team sports. Are you two on teams?"

"I play basketball," Alice answers. "*He* wouldn't try out."

"Why would I?" says Mickey.

The only thing Mickey dislikes more than playing sports is being asked why he doesn't play sports.

"Oh, I don't know," says Felicity. "Collegiality. Exercise. Fun?"

"They already throw enough balls at me," says Mickey.

He ducks as a prickly green ball—a cactus basketball—nearly hits him in the head. "See?"

"What game are they playing?" asks Felicity.

"Dodge ball?" guesses Mickey.

"But . . . *cactus* dodge ball?" Alice shudders in her brother's palm.

More prickly green balls—cactus soccer balls—whizz by.

The desert is now roiling with cactuses, all pelting one another. Even the saguaros are getting in on the action, tossing cactus balls from the sidelines.

"Well, don't just stand there—run!" yells Alice, wrapping an arm around each side of her brother's wrist.

But he doesn't run. He can't. He is too overwhelmed. Is this what the invisible boy was warning him about? How do you stay "chill" when you're in the middle of a cactus war?

"Incoming!" warns Felicity as another round of the cactus basketballs rains down around them.

An enormous prickle-ball narrowly misses Mickey's ear. Instead, it clips the flyhouse on the edge of her roof.

"Ohhhhhh!" Felicity cries as she goes spinning above Mickey's head.

"Mickey, move!" shouts Alice.

"Sorry!"

At last, Mickey starts to run, weaving this way and that to avoid collision with the chollas.

He forgets to run like a robot or not like a robot. He doesn't know whether he's moving his arms or not moving his arms.

All he can think about is dodging cacti. Or cactuses. Or whatever you call them.

Luckily, the enraged desert flora are totally bent on

destroying one another, and hardly aware of the non-plant-based strangers in their midst.

Or so it seems.

Just as Mickey breaks free of the melee, there is a sudden, eerie silence.

Mickey turns to see the two teams joined together—a single army of chollas, all pointing in his direction.

21.

Ow! Ow! Ow!

"THERE HE IS!"

"GET HIM!"

Dozens of cactus balls fly toward Mickey. They fall on all sides. There is no escaping them now.

A ball grazes his ear. Another grazes his arm. Another hits him in the leg.

"Ow! Ow! Ow!"

"DON'T YOU WANT TO PLAY, WITTLE MICKEY?"

"YEAH, YOU AFWAID OF A WITTLE BALL?"

"POOR WITTLE MICKEY!"

"They really *are* playing dodge ball!" says Alice, covering her face.

"Yep. And now they're aiming at me!" Mickey says, running again. "This world is just like the regular world, only worse!"

"LOOK AT HIM—THE WUSS!"

"GONNA GO RUN TO YOUR DADDY?"

"WHERE'S YOUR RAINBOW UNICORN NOW?"

"You want my advice?" asks Alice.

"No."

"I do!" Felicity shouts from above. "Please."

"Get away from the edge of the field—you need space on all sides," says Alice. "And don't crouch down! It only makes you more of a target. Dodge Ball 101."

Mickey takes her advice and runs at his full height, closer to the center of the field.

"DON'T LET HIM GET AWAY!"

"GET HIM!"

"GET HIM!"

Shouting and hollering, the chollas chase after Mickey, and send another volley of cactus balls his way. "To the left!" Alice calls out, and Mickey lunges left.

"Now the right!" she shouts again, and he rolls right.

"This is so exciting!" Felicity shrieks, and he keeps running.

And running. And running.

Mickey doesn't stop running until he is out of breath and there is a horrible cramp in his side. He doubles over, panting.

His sister dangles from a finger before righting herself.

"Pretty good, little bro."

"Thanks," says Mickey. "And, um, thanks for the advice."

She smiles. "I'm your big sister, remember? I'm not

going to let some thorny green wannabe bullies get you."

Behind them, in the distance, the chollas are now little more than dots on the field. Furious, they jump up and down, yelling familiar middle school obscenities.

"Do they really throw balls at you at school?" asks Alice, watching the chollas.

"Only every day. It's like a tradition."

Clenching his teeth, Mickey pulls tiny cholla needles from his forearms.

"At least you're fast," Alice says, climbing up his sleeve to avoid being plucked along with the needles.

"Huh?" Mickey thinks she's kidding. He is not used to receiving compliments about his running or . . . dodging.

"Like, really fast. Maybe you should run track."

"You really think so?" Mickey almost smiles at her. Almost.

"Sure," says Alice, reaching his shoulder again. "You should try out. I can ask Sean to give you a few pointers."

Car-Boy's name lands like a cactus ball in his gut.

He looks away from his sister, toward the dry desert horizon. "No thanks."

"Why not?"

"Because."

Because he calls me names, Mickey is about to say. *Because he* . . . What is that word? Mickey can't remember what it is that Car-Boy says that upsets him so much. He just remembers how it makes him feel.

It's so quiet, Mickey can hear the buzzing wings of the flyhouse.

"Middle school sucks," says his sister with unexpected vehemence.

"Sure does." Mickey keeps his eyes on Felicity, though he can feel Alice pacing across his shoulder.

"It gets better in high school."

"Does it?"

"Well, sometimes . . . Where are we anyway?" asks Alice, changing the subject.

"Hold on—"

As Alice grabs on to his earlobe for support, Mickey stands fully upright for the first time since escaping the chollas.

They are now so far from the soccer field that he doesn't recognize anything around them. They could be in the middle of any desert, anywhere in the world.

"We're lost," says Mickey. "That's where we are."

22.

M is for *west.*

"Everything really is gone, isn't it?" asks Alice.

Alice has climbed all the way to the top of her brother's head. Holding a handful of hair in each hand to steady herself, she peers into the distance, like a ship captain looking for shore.

"Yep. And I have no idea how to get to Mad or Bad or anywhere else. And by the way, that hurts."

"Sorry." Alice relaxes her grip—slightly.

"Are there no landmarks to help you navigate?" asks Felicity, circling nervously above. "An Eiffel Tower? A Taj Mahal? A Mount Fuji?"

"Um . . . there's Double Mountain," says Mickey. "Or there used to be. You can usually see it from school. But not now."

Double Mountain—so-called because of its two, similarly shaped peaks—is the biggest mountain in the area, but it is hard to see when the air is smoggy or hazy. Or, apparently, when half the world has disappeared.

Of course, it may have disappeared too. Replaced by Bubble Mountain perhaps?

Mickey opens the map again.

From atop his head, Alice looks down at the confusing jumble of lines and circles. "That long line. Isn't that the arroyo? It looks like it takes us right through Mad."

"Okay, but how do we get to the arroyo?"

"Just like you do every day! It's west of your school. So we go west."

"Right," says Mickey, relieved for once to hear his sister's authoritative tone. "Wait. Which way is west?"

"Isn't that what your compass is for?" asks Alice, pointing.

As always, a red compass dangles from the keychain clipped to Mickey's belt loop.

"It's just a toy. You know, from a pack of gum."

"Another package from the king, huh? And it doesn't work?"

"No . . . Well, I don't really know." Mickey blushes, realizing he's never checked to see if the compass is accurate.

He detaches his keychain and brings the compass to eye level.

"It's spinning at least." He squints, confused. "So, like, west is always *W,* right?"

"Last time I checked," says Alice. "Do you mind keeping your head level? I'm getting head-sick again."

"Well, do directions ever have other names? Or initials? Could west be *M*?"

"Maybe in a foreign language."

"No language I know," says Felicity. Her tone implies that if she doesn't know a language, the language isn't worth knowing. "Is it possible you're looking at the letter upside down?"

"Oh, wait, yeah, I guess I was." Embarrassed, Mickey cranes his neck, looking at the compass from the other direction. "It must be a *W*."

"Whichever way the needle is pointing is north," says his sister. "West is always to the left of the needle."

"How do you know that?" asks Mickey, genuinely impressed.

Alice shrugs. "Girl Scouts? Life? That's just the way compasses are."

"Okay, well, anyway, *M* is that way," says Mickey, turning to his left. "I mean west is. *M* for *west*. Well, you know what I mean."

"No, I don't, but let's go anyway. Now. Because I am so over being little," says Alice, tugging on a handful of Mickey's hair.

"Ow!"

The flyhouse rises in the air, buzzing happily. "I'm so glad you two found each other. Family is so important."

Sister and brother groan in unison.

"Go." Alice points. "West."

Mickey starts walking, still staring at his compass.

He was looking at it the right way the first time, he realizes. The *M* is an *M*, not a *W*. If it were a *W*, the other letters would be upside down as well, and they aren't.

In fact, only one of the usual four letters is on the face of the compass. Instead of *N, S, E,* and *W* (north, south, east, and west), the letters are *M, B, S,* and *G*.

Absorbed in his compass, he stubs his toe on a rock. "Gah!"

His sister flies up from his scalp as if she's riding a bronco.

"Hey, watch out!" she exclaims, holding tight to his hair. "You're carrying precious cargo."

"Sorry," says Mickey. "This compass is kind of wonky."

An idea suddenly occurring to him, he pulls the map out of his pants pocket and compares it to the compass.

"Hey, are those footprints behind you?" Alice asks.

"Yeah, mine," Mickey answers without looking up.

Maybe the letters don't represent directions at all. Maybe they represent the four states of the Anti-World.

M. B. S. G.

Mad. Bad. Sad. Glad.

"No, *next* to yours," Alice insists.

Mickey glances over his shoulder. There appears to be a second trail of footprints—uncannily similar to his own—in the sand next to his.

"I have four feet," he says, picking up his pace. "You never noticed?"

"Very funny."

The second set of footprints stops for a moment, allowing Mickey to get ahead. Then it resumes from a safer distance.

The see-through boy is following him again.

part three:

mad

23.

Ewwww!

Whatever *M* stands for—a direction, a state of mind, or something else altogether—Mickey, Alice, and Felicity are heading toward it.

Is it the right direction? Mickey doesn't know. How do you know if you're going *to* Mad. Or just *going* mad?

But suppose they get to Mad, and from there to Bad—to Bubble Mountain. Yes, the priority has to be getting Alice back home and back to normal. But does Mickey have to go home with her? Does he *want* to?

That's the question that's plaguing him.

What if his sister remembers what happened to her? What if *everyone* learns what Mickey has done?

He will be the boy who made the world disappear. An outcast. A monster.

Not the best conditions for a homecoming.

Meanwhile, Alice has abandoned her post on the top

of his head, climbing down his left ear to his left shoulder.

"A little less bumpy down here."

She looks up at his nose in alarm. "That is the biggest booger I've ever seen! It's like this huge green alien pod!"

"Here—you can help me pick it out." Mickey bends his head toward her, so she is almost touching his nostril.

"Ewwwwww! I better take a picture. Nobody's going to believe this."

Before he can move his nose away, Alice expertly snaps a photo.

Fascinated, she stares at her brother's image in her phone. "Have you seen your pores? I have to teach you about skin care. You're going to be a teenager soon. Do you know what that means?"

"That you suddenly think you're really cool and go out with an older guy who's a total troglodyte?" The words come out before Mickey can stop them.

Alice gives him a look. A hurt look. "No, it means zits and blackheads."

"Children, children," scolds Felicity, hovering over them like an overly protective nanny, alert to any looming disagreement.

"Hey, I know—you can ride in my pocket," says Mickey, as a peace-making gesture. "That way you won't have to look at me anymore."

"Your pants pocket?!"

"No! My hoodie pocket. Seriously, I think you'll be more comfortable."

On her knees, Alice leans over the edge of Mickey's shoulder and eyes the hoodie's pockets (there are two) warily. "Promise there's nothing gross in there?"

"Besides my old wads of gum?"

"You keep them?!"

Mickey snickers. "Well, not separately. I roll them all together into a ball."

"Mickey!" Alice shouts. "Disgusting! And totally TMI."

"Just like a dung beetle—how fascinating!" says Felicity. "Do you re-chew the balls when they reach a certain size or do you let them grow indefinitely?"

"I was kidding!"

"Well, excuse me for being curious!" The flyhouse flies away in a huff.

(For the record, Mickey wasn't kidding; he has been working on his ball of gum for months. But the last time he saw it, it was hidden in a drawer, not in his hoodie.)

As carefully as he can, Mickey deposits his sister in the right-hand pocket of his sweatshirt, a safe distance from the Anti-Book, which remains tucked inside the left-hand pocket.

"Better?"

Her response is muffled, but he clearly hears the words *smelly, sandy,* and *like a sleeping bag.*

Alice wriggles around in his pocket, tickling his stomach.

"Yes, better!" she says, peeking her head out. "Hey, I know where we are now. There's the arroyo. But where's . . . the bridge is gone! Just like you . . ." She trails off.

"Just like I said, yeah," says Mickey grimly.

A moment later, they stand at the edge of the arroyo, where the road now simply ends as if it has been sliced in half.

Disgruntled, Alice nods toward the bronze plaque plastered to a stone pedestal. "That used to say *Arroyo Perdido Dam*."

MAD DAM
ANGER MANAGEMENT
AND EMOTIONAL FLOOD CONTROL

"And is it because of my size, or does the water look different too?"

Mickey looks down into the arroyo.

"No, you're right. It's like a full-on river now. And sort of darker and rougher."

And, he can't help thinking, angrier.

The flyhouse alights on the plaque and examines it. "Did you ever notice that *MAD* is *DAM* backward?" she asks.

"Not exactly," Alice says.

Yes, exactly, Mickey says to himself. Backward—like everything else right now.

The wheel of a car floats by, bobbing and spinning in

the churning water. Mickey thinks he recognizes it as a wheel from Car-Boy's Camaro. But how could the Camaro's wheel have wound up in the river?

Felicity buzzes worriedly around them as the tire disappears from view. "Do you two hear that?"

"Hear what?" asks Alice. Tense, she grips the top edge of Mickey's sweatshirt pocket as if it were a guardrail on a balcony.

"An animal in distress, I think. Of course, I haven't met many animals yet, so I can't say for sure."

Mickey listens until he hears it too. A sharp, shrill noise in the distance.

"Sounds more like a fire alarm," he says. "Or a police siren."

"Um, I doubt there are any police around," says Alice. "Unless they have cactus police."

The sound gets louder. Whatever it is is coming closer.

Soon, it is almost unbearable. Piercing and insistent. And at the same time whining and desperate.

Alice covers her ears with her hands. "It's horrible."

And then they see it heading toward them over the desert.

Screaming.

The sound is a scream.

24.

A walking oxymoron.

The screamer looks, in general, like a person, but larger and rounder than any person Mickey has ever seen.

This person—or person-like thing—moves rapidly and erratically, like a balloon tossed by the wind. Which is all the weirder because there is no wind.

"Um, I think we should go," says Alice.

"Yeah," Mickey agrees, but he doesn't move.

The screamer comes closer.

Why does the screamer look so familiar?

"Don't freeze up on me again! Run!" Alice yelps. "Why aren't you running? You're fast, remember?"

Then, without warning, the screamer stops about ten feet from where Mickey stands.

"Wait. Don't move." Alice leans over the edge of the hoodie pocket, almost falling out. "Is that who I think it is?"

Mickey stares in confusion. "What's *he* doing here?"

"He's always here," says Alice. "I mean, he always was before . . . It *is* Adam, isn't it?"

It certainly appears to be Adam. AKA Mime-Boy.

He wears the same striped shirt, the same white makeup, the same red plastic carnation in his buttonhole. Even the beret has reappeared—on his head.

He resembles Mime-Boy in all respects but one: Unlike the skinny guy that tormented Mickey, this fellow is bizarrely bloated. He looks as though he has been pumped up with helium and might float away at any second.

Mickey can't help feeling a little sorry for him.

"Adam?" Alice calls out tentatively.

Without looking at them, Mime-Boy bows to an unseen audience, then pats the air and pretends it's a wall. He tugs on an invisible rope, until an invisible partner lets go. He juggles two imaginary balls, then three, then four, then drops them one after another. He does all the things he usually does, all the things mimes usually do.

Except usually mimes do these things in silence.

He, on the other hand, is screaming.

"Oh, my—a screaming mime!" exclaims Felicity. "He's a walking oxymoron."

It is not a normal human scream. It is more like the cry of a cat fighting in an alley. Or the cry of a woodland animal caught in a hunter's trap. It comes from somewhere deep inside, and he seems unable to control it.

"Adam?!?" Alice tries again.

It is hard to tell whether he hears Alice shouting his

name. Although he doesn't respond, his scream becomes momentarily quizzical, as if he is reminded of something but is unsure of what.

"Stop screaming!" Alice yells. "Tell us what you want!"

But he won't or can't stop. He keeps repeating his routine. *Build wall . . . Tug rope . . . Juggle balls . . . Build wall . . .*

"Do you think he wants our help?" frets Alice.

Usually, he just wants to make fun of me, Mickey thinks.

"A–dam this is A–lice and Mick–ey," Felicity says, carefully enunciating each word. "Your friends are ve-ry concerned a-bout you. Do you un-der-stand?"

Still screaming, Mime-Boy looks blankly at them for a moment. Until a flicker of recognition crosses his face.

He makes a few exaggerated chewing motions with his mouth, then leans his head back and starts blowing a big imaginary bubble.

"Bubble gum!" Alice exclaims. "He knows it's you, Mickey!"

"Uh-huh," says Mickey, red-faced.

Mime-Boy opens his hands wider and wider to show the bubble growing bigger and bigger. Until, suddenly—pop!—he staggers backward and starts peeling imaginary gum from his face.

He points at Mickey and laughs mirthlessly.

"Adam, stop making fun of Mickey for a second," says Alice. "Just tell us, do you know where Sean is? Do you know what's happened to everyone?"

But Mime-Boy is not listening to the three-inch-tall girl

in Mickey's pocket; he is staring directly at Mickey, his expression ominous.

"Wh-what?" asks Mickey, chilled.

Mime-Boy points upward with his index finger.

"Something about the sky?" Alice guesses. "A cloud? The sun?"

Mime-Boy shakes his head. Still screaming, he counts on his fingers, then points upward again.

Alice keeps guessing. "One minute? The number one?"

Mime-Boy nods. Number one it is.

Next, he places two fingers in the crook of his opposing elbow.

"One elbow?" Alice suggests. "A one-armed person . . . ?"

Mickey is certain Mime-Boy is threatening him with something terrible. Neither Mime-Boy nor Car-Boy has ever physically hurt Mickey, but Mickey always sensed that it was just a matter of time.

He should have run away when he had the chance.

"Wait—are you playing charades?" asks Alice. "Like, first word, two syllables?"

Mime-Boy nods again, grateful to be understood.

"How delightful!" says Felicity. "I've always wanted to play charades."

"Talk to Mickey," says Alice. "He lives for charades."

"I do not," says Mickey unconvincingly.

Last New Year's Eve, their family game lasted all night, finally ending when Alice pointed to herself and Mickey immediately shouted *Despicable Me!*"

Everyone laughed. Even Alice. Even Mickey's dad.

For a second, Mickey remembers how good it felt.

A day later, his parents announced their separation.

"What's the first syllable, Adam?" asks Alice now.

Mime-Boy starts looking in all directions as if watching something fly around.

"*Bird*?" Alice suggests.

He squeezes his fingers together. Something smaller.

Felicity narrows all eighteen of her windowpane eyes. "A fly? You're not talking about me, are you?"

He pinches his arm and winces, as if he has been bitten or stung.

"*Mosquito*?" hazards Alice.

"Too many syllables," says Felicity.

"*Bee*?" suggests Mickey.

Mime-Boy nods vehemently.

The flyhouse buzzes with satisfaction. "So the first syllable is *bee*. I knew I'd like this game! What's the second syllable?"

Mime-Boy looks around again, his face wrinkling in confusion.

Mickey watches him apprehensively as the others continue to throw out ideas.

"You lost something?"

"You have amnesia?"

"You're lost?"

"The word *lost*?" Mickey asks.

Mime-Boy shrugs and wiggles his hand.

Lost is close, but it's not right.

He opens his hands and looks questioningly at them.

"You need directions . . . *Map?*" Felicity guesses.

He makes a beckoning gesture. Keep guessing.

Felicity: "Where is it?"

Alice: "Where am I going?"

Mickey: "Where—the word *where,* is that it?"

Mime-Boy nods.

"So we've got *bee-where,*" concludes Mickey. "The first word is *beware!*"

"See, I knew you'd figure it out, Mickey!" Thrilled, Alice almost jumps out of her brother's sweatshirt. "He wants to warn you about something. But what? Adam, what should Mickey beware of?"

Mime-Boy holds up two fingers. Second word. He places them in his elbow. Two syllables. Then he puts his index finger to his lips.

"Be quiet?" guesses Alice. "We should be quiet? Or *quiet* is the second word?"

He shakes his head.

"Shh? The word is *shh?*"

"No, it's two syllables," says Mickey. "So *shh* is the beginning of the word? *Beware shh*-something . . . ?"

But Mime-Boy has stopped playing charades, and there is a new look of fear on his face.

His scream gets louder and louder.

25.

Exactamundo!

Beware shh-blank?

Is Alice right? Mickey assumed Mime-Boy was threatening him, but maybe Mime-Boy was trying to warn him.

With his bloated face and endless screaming, he certainly looks and sounds like the harbinger of something terrible.

Felicity flies in agitated circles above them. "That poor man! What are we going to do?"

"I don't know—I can't stand it!" Alice buries herself in Mickey's pocket.

"Psst. Do the thing."

"Huh?" says Mickey, squinting his eyes.

The see-through boy is leaning against a mesquite tree. He looks so relaxed, he could have been there all day.

Was it his presence that scared Mime-Boy?

"The book, dude. Use it."

His breezy tone makes Mickey apoplectic. "Have you been with us this whole time?" Mickey whispers furiously. "Because you might have warned me that some psycho cactuses were going to try to kill me! And now—"

"And now there's that screamer over there. You want to get rid of him, right?"

"Well, we want him to stop screaming, yeah."

"Exactamundo! You want to put him out of his misery."

"Mickey, are you talking to yourself again?" asks Alice from inside her fleece-lined hideaway.

"No."

She peeks her head out. "You are, aren't you?"

"Yeah. Sorry. Just psyching myself up," Mickey says quickly. "I think I know how to get Mime-Boy, I mean Adam, to stop screaming."

"Good. Hurry." Alice slides back into Mickey's pocket.

"You do know how, right?" Mickey whispers.

"No, *you* know how," says the boy. "He's a scrime. Write it down."

"He's a what?"

"A SCRIME. Like *CRIME* with an *S*. Or *SLIME* with a *C-R*. Well, like *SLIME* with a *C-R* and no *L*. Well, you get the point. *SCREAM* plus *MIME* equals *SCRIME*."

Mickey glances back at Mime-Boy, who is still screaming. And still staring. His face is so red that he looks like he might explode.

"The scrime is an anti-character," continues the see-through boy. "You're the anti-hero. Make it happen."

Mickey gapes at him. "I'm an . . . anti-hero?"

The boy nods. "Yup. It's just like a superhero. Well, except for the super part. And the hero part. It's more like the opposite. I guess you could say you're an un-super villain. What!!!"

"Gee, thanks."

"Just messing with you, bro. Chill. But for real, use the book. Write. I know you can do it. It's your un-super power. What!!! There I go again!" The boy laughs. He really does crack himself up.

Alice reemerges and looks around suspiciously. "Are you still psyching yourself up? I thought you were going to make him stop."

"What? Oh, yeah, sorry," says Mickey.

"Quit stalling and write," insists the see-through boy. "*S-C-R-I-M-E.*"

Alice doesn't react. She still can't hear him.

The boy's right, Mickey thinks. I'm stalling. Mickey doesn't want to reveal the Anti-Book's power to his sister, whether super, un-super, or otherwise.

Then again, she's bound to find out about the Anti-Book sooner or later.

"Scrime . . . Scrime . . . Scrime . . . Scrime . . ." the boy chants, louder and louder.

Reluctantly, Mickey pulls the book out of his pocket and fishes around for his pencil.

"The Anti-Book? What's that?" his sister asks from the opposite pocket.

"My journal."

"Your journal?" Alice looks up at Mickey, incredulous. "I mean, that's cool—I'm glad you're expressing your feelings and everything. But *now*? Really?"

Mickey swallows and writes:

scrime

It doesn't work. Or rather, it doesn't work right away. And it doesn't work in the same way it did the first time around.

The scrime doesn't disappear, but the screaming stops, replaced by something more like the whistle of a teakettle.

Alice looks searchingly at him. "Adam, are you okay?"

He stares back with a grave expression. For a second time, he mimes a sting on his arm and looks around in confusion. *Bee-where* . . .

This time, however, he doesn't put his finger to his lips, he merely points at the see-through boy.

"What are you pointing at?" Alice asks. "Beware what?"

Before the scrime can answer, he starts shriveling like a deflating balloon. Just as he's about to collapse to the ground, he lets out a final scream and shoots into the sky.

They watch, dumbstruck, as he spirals through the air.

He sails out of sight in the direction, Mickey guesses, of Double Mountain. Or Bubble Mountain.

"Dude, that was so awesome, it was like the sum of awe! You just popped him, and he went—" The see-through boy whistles and makes a spiral in the air with a finger. "What!!!"

Mickey flushes at the compliment. Then he sees his sister's horrified expression.

"What just happened? What did you do to him?"

"Nothing," says Mickey immediately. "I'm sure he's fine. That probably wasn't even him, right? Just the Anti-World version."

"What about me? Am I just the Anti-World version of your sister? Are you going to shoot me into the sky too?"

Oops. The see-through boy grimaces in sympathy. Mickey walked right into that one.

"You're not my anti-sister, you're my . . . re-sister," improvises Mickey. "You're just like a new version. Not an anti-version."

"Ha! Nice one!" says the boy. "She's the re-sistance!"

"You're the re-sistance," Mickey repeats.

A stony expression on her face, Alice holds out her tiny hand to Mickey. "Let me see it."

"What?"

"Your journal."

He forces a laugh. "Why? You think there's a red eject button in there?"

"Let. Me. See. It."

"Okay. Here." He shows her the Anti-Book without opening it. It's bigger than she is.

Mickey can feel himself sweating under his shirt. He's never been very good at lying to his sister, and, unfortunately, her new compact size doesn't make it any easier.

She points up at her brother's nose. "If you had anything to do with all of this, I will kill you!"

The see-through boy snickers. "Uh-oh!"

Mickey darts him a look. This is his fault.

"Just get us to Bubble Mountain or Trouble Mountain or whatever it's called," says Alice, staring into the distance from Mickey's pocket. "Before anybody else explodes."

"Which way?" Mickey whispers.

"The way you've been going." Grinning, the boy points up the arroyo. "Up that creek without a paddle."

He starts walking, beckoning Mickey to follow.

26.

What!!!

"So what are you? A ghost?" Mickey asks in a low voice.

Still angry at her brother, Alice has moved out of the snug confines of his pocket and is now perched in the hood of his sweatshirt, cross-legged, with her back to Mickey. She has put on her yellow headphones, shutting out not only her brother, but the entire Anti-World.

Leaving Mickey free to question the elusive boy walking beside him.

"A ghost? That would be lit! Ooooowoooh . . ." The boy makes ghostly sounds. "Did I scare you?" He laughs.

"Then what are you really?" Mickey asks. "Or who, I mean."

"Shadow, at your service." The boy bows, offering an ironic smile. "But you can call me Shad. That's Shadow, hold the *o* and the *w*. As in, *or* and *what*! As in, *Am I cool or what? What!!!*"

Mickey smiles back, uncertain how to react.

"So, uh, Shad, are you a, what did you call it, an anti-character too?"

"Sure. Practically everyone here is! We're in the Anti-World, aren't we?" Shadow matches Mickey's stride, step for step. "That little critter sitting in your hood?—she's your anti-sister. Just like she said. That flying cuckoo clock up there?—an anti-housefly."

Mickey looks up at Felicity flying above them. She waves a wing at Mickey, still seemingly unaware of Shadow.

"And what about you? Who are you the anti of?"

"Oh, I'm just Shadow the shadow," says Shadow. "Not really anti-anybody at the moment."

"Okay, then who are you the shadow of?" Mickey persists.

"Nobody. Yet." Shadow's lips curl into a half smile. "I'm more of a *fore*shadow, you could say."

Mickey squints. The sun is shining directly on Shadow, and Mickey can make out his features more clearly than before. Like Mickey, he has longish hair that hangs over his eyes, but unlike Mickey, whose hair and eyes are brown, Shadow's eyes are a watery gray, and his hair so light, it's almost white.

"Foreshadow? That's like a prediction, right?" Mickey asks. "So what are you foreshadowing?"

"So many questions! It's like they say in the movies: If I told you, I'd have to kill you." Shadow gives him an exaggeratedly evil chuckle. "Mwahahaha . . . What!!!"

Mickey laughs half-heartedly.

"Well, can you at least tell me what makes an anti? At first, I thought everything here was the opposite of a thing. Or maybe the reverse. Or the inverse . . ."

"Well, sure, but it could also be a kickflip. Or a hardflip. Or a backside one-eighty . . ."

Mickey frowns. "Isn't that, um, skateboarding?"

"Or a triple axel combination . . ."

"That's ice-skating!"

"See, now you're getting it. Ice-skating is anti-skateboarding. What!!!"

This time, Mickey laughs along with Shadow.

"Seriously, though. If anti isn't opposite, what is it?"

They are still walking along the arroyo, but with every step it looks less and less like the arroyo Mickey has known all his life. Even the trickle of water at the bottom, the trickle that turned into a river—it has switched direction, and the current is now flowing ever so slightly uphill.

"Think of it as the negative of a negative," says Shadow.

"The negative of a negative is a positive," says Mickey. He remembers that much from school.

"Depends on how you define it," says Shadow judiciously. "Pro tip: Don't define it."

Alice removes her headphones. "You're talking to yourself again!"

"Sorry!" says Mickey with a start. "I didn't think you could hear me."

"Are you sure you're not going crazy? Hearing voices or whatever? Because if you are, I need to know. So I can find a new hoodie to ride in—and someone else to get me home!"

Mickey looks over his shoulder, to where his tiny red-haired sister is sitting in his hood. "Little Red Riding Hood—that's what I should call you!"

Shadow laughs. "Good one."

Alice looks at Mickey oddly.

"What?" he asks.

"Is there somebody else here or not?"

"What do you mean?"

"Like somebody invisible."

"I told you I was joking about that," says Mickey, suddenly reluctant to share Shadow with her.

"I just heard him laughing."

"I think you're hallucinating."

"I think you're lying."

Alice stares at her brother.

"Yeah, I'm sorry, you're right, I'm lying," says Mickey sarcastically. "In reality, there's an invisible boy who's been leading us around the Anti-World for the last twenty minutes."

Alice studies the trail—or rather two trails—in the desert behind them. "Look, somebody else's footprints again! They're his, aren't they?"

Walking beside Mickey, Shadow shrugs. Busted.

Mickey notices that the see-through boy is no longer

quite as see-through as he was. He's a bit denser or thicker or more solid. Still translucent, but less transparent.

At this rate, Alice will soon be able to see him.

"Oh, what the heck," says Shadow. He cups his hands and yells, "Yo, Alice! What's up, girl?"

Startled, Alice almost falls out of Mickey's hoodie. "Okay, that time I heard him for sure."

"His name is Shadow," says Mickey, giving up the fight.

Alice squints in Shadow's direction. "Shadow? Where?"

"Here!" Shadow waves, but she still doesn't see him.

Felicity flies down for a look, but she can't seem to see Shadow either.

"I must say, this seems highly irregular," the flyhouse says. "There's nothing else you're not telling us, is there, Mickey?"

"Yeah, he's not like some evil fairy godmother, is he?" asks Alice. "Are you sure he didn't do all this? To the world? To me?"

Mickey shakes his head. "No. Course not. He's a nice guy," says Mickey, hoping he's not stretching the truth too much.

"I'll be the judge of that." Alice waves to the air. "Hey Shadow! I can't see you, but . . . Hi!"

"Hi yourself."

Alice looks at her brother. "Did he say something?"

"I said, Hi yourself!" Shadow shouts.

"Oh, there you are," says Alice in Shadow's direction. "So, are you just air or do you have a face and a body?"

"Sure, arms, legs, nose, everything." Shadow steps closer. "Trust me. I'm the cutest guy you've ever not seen. What!!!"

Alice snorts. "You don't sound cute; you sound obnoxious."

She tilts her head. "Actually, if I look closely, I can sort of see you. You remind me of someone . . ."

"Must be someone super awesome," says Shadow.

"Yeah . . . no. You must remind me of air. I don't know any see-through people."

"Oh, now I see him too, I think!" says the flyhouse, buzzing curiously around them. "Is invisibility very common where you're from, Alice?"

Alice laughs. "Not very."

Mickey looks from Alice to Shadow to Alice again as they continue walking. He is relieved that Shadow is no longer a secret, but he can't help resenting how at ease his sister seems in Shadow's presence.

She has never been intimidated by strangers—it's one of her gifts. But an invisible stranger? Wouldn't that unnerve anyone?

Suddenly, Shadow stands in Mickey's way. "Quick—don't think! Your dream car—is it an SUV, sports car, pickup truck, minivan . . . ?"

"Uh, sports car, I guess?"

Mickey is annoyed to realize he is picturing Car-Boy's Camaro. Couldn't his dream car be something else?

Shadow appraises him. "Okay. It's a reach, but I like it."

"For what?"

"Your new car. You didn't think we were going to keep walking forever, did you? Not all the way to Bubble Mountain! We're going shopping, bro. Check it out—"

Shadow points to a low-slung building overlooked by a giant neon robot in a cowboy hat, holding a blinking lasso.

ROBO JOE'S
AUTO RODEO
"Cool your heels with a new set of wheels!"

"But I don't have any money," Mickey protests.

Shadow waves his hand dismissively. "No worries, man. I know Joe. He'll make us a deal."

"Plus, Mickey doesn't have a license," Alice volunteers. "Or know how to drive."

"Oh, Joe's cars practically drive themselves," says Shadow. "He'll be fine. You can help him navigate."

Felicity, who, like Alice, now seems to hear Shadow perfectly well, buzzes disapprovingly. "As the youngest but most mature party involved, I must object. This plan sounds unwise, not to mention unsafe."

Flying close to Mickey's ear, she murmurs, "How can you trust someone you can't see? You don't even know him."

Mickey eyes Shadow uncertainly. "One question: Why are you helping with all this?"

"What do you mean? I'm all about you, Mickey. We're like *this,* you and me." He holds up two fingers and brings them together. "Best buddies, right?"

Mickey swallows. It's been a long time since he has had a best buddy, or any buddy at all. And a part of him—a small, buried, barely acknowledged part—is grateful to hear he has one.

Even if they've only just met. Even if the buddy is only half-visible.

"Short version: Don't look a gift horse in the mouth," says Shadow. "Or a gift car, either."

Mickey shrugs uneasily. "Okay, if you say so."

"I say so," says Shadow. "One warning about Joe, though. He's very, er, well-armed."

"You mean with weapons?!" asks Alice, alarmed.

"Not that kind of armed. You'll see."

Nervous but curious, they follow Shadow down the street to Robo Joe's.

As they approach, horns blare from the used car lot, greeting the new customers. Or, possibly, warning them away.

27.

Wheels, deals, and automobiles!

"So that's what he meant by well-armed!" says Alice as Robo Joe walks jerkily toward them.

Just like the neon version, the robot car salesman is dressed as a cowboy in boots and hat. He even has a lasso tied to his waist.

There is one glaring difference, however: The actual, 3-D robot has four arms, not two. The arms move back and forth in creaky unison, straight and stiff, like the arms of a tin soldier.

Unconsciously, Mickey touches the Anti-Book.

Robot arms, he wrote. And now there's an *armed robot.*

"Well, I'll be a monkey's motorcycle! If it ain't Mr. Shadow himself! You lookin' for some new wheels today, partner?"

As Robo Joe tips his hat to Shadow, Mickey sees that

he's made entirely of car parts: a muffler for a head, axles for legs, exhaust pipes for arms, and a mystifying mechanical jumble for the rest.

"Say, what do you call a wheel that's all worn out?" asks Robo Joe, not waiting for an answer to his first question.

"Tired?" guesses Shadow.

"Now, now, what did I tell you about spoiling my jokes?" the robot complains.

Shadow grins. "Can't spoil a joke that's already rotten."

"Touché!" Robo Joe raises one of his four arms to his mouth and takes a puff on a spark-plug pipe. A spray of orange sparks is released, and he coughs up a cloud of black smoke.

"Got anything that'll make it to Bubble Mountain without blowing a gasket?" says Shadow, fanning the smoke away. "I told my buddy here you'd make us a deal."

"*Steal* is more like it, knowing you. You think I'm made of money?" Joe winks at Mickey.

Mickey stares back. Joe's eyes, at least, *are* made of money. Silver dollars, to be precise.

"So which of these beauties is calling your name, cowboy?" With a sweeping gesture, Joe indicates the vehicles behind him. They are arranged in a circle, like wagons in the old west.

"Um . . . I . . . I dunno," Mickey stammers.

The "beauties" are a motley bunch, pieced together as if at random from old cars, trucks, tractors, and assorted machinery. Their engines rumble ominously.

Mickey can't imagine buying any of them, let alone driving one.

"There's not a lemon in the bunch," Joe declares. "Scout's honor."

By now Alice has crawled out from Mickey's sweatshirt hood and is sitting on his shoulder, blinking in the sunlight.

"Well, hello, little lady," says Joe with a creaky bow. "Maybe you can help this fellow choose a car."

Alice wrinkles her nose. "Is someone wearing perfume? It smells good, but it's pretty strong."

Mickey sniffs. A sweet, flowery smell is wafting around the used car lot.

"Nice, huh?" Robo Joe smiles at them. "That's Eau de Voiture. The Perfume Wagon's signature scent."

He nods toward a station wagon with an oddly protruding hood and two nostril-like holes in the grill.

Mickey stares in surprise. "That's Mom's car!" he says to his sister. "The Pee-ew Wagon!"

"And now it's the Perfume Wagon!" says Alice. "How perfect."

As they watch, aghast, the wagon's nostrils quiver and its front fender seems to twitch. Suddenly, the hood flies open and releases a forceful, floral-smelling gust of air—an automotive sneeze! Next comes an aromatic burst of smoke from the wagon's tailpipe—an automotive fart!

Mickey waves away the sickly sweet fumes.

"Now that one is a special case," says Joe. "She's a bit gassy—pun very much intended—but she's got no interest in gasoline at all. Keeps trying to nibble on plants, like a cow. Can you believe it?"

Mickey nods. Yes, he can believe it.

When his mother first converted her wagon from gasoline to "plant-based fuel," she and Mickey would drive from fast-food restaurant to fast-food restaurant, collecting used cooking oil to power the car. His mother planned to start a business selling diesel engine conversion kits, and Mickey brainstormed names with her as they drove. *Veggie-car. Bio-auto. Fry-mobile.*

Sure, the car always smelled of French fries, but it was fun. For a while.

Over time, the smell of fries turned into something worse, and his mom's business plans evaporated. She tried to sell the wagon back to the dealership, but they said she'd ruined it. (What was their name? Could it be Auto Rodeo?) The car became an embarrassment. Mickey didn't ride in it unless he had to, and even then he would slink down in his seat so no one could see him.

Of course, compared to how the car looks now, it was positively normal-looking back then. And even at its stinkiest, the car wasn't unbearable. Why couldn't he have just laughed about it?

Maybe he can make up for it now.

"What about that one?" he asks.

"Are you sure?" says Felicity, who has just appeared

above Mickey's head. "Isn't there one that smells more like, oh . . ."

"Poop?" suggests Shadow.

Mickey guiltily stifles a laugh.

Felicity narrows her windowpane eyes. "I hope that wasn't some sort of slur."

"That wagon isn't going anywhere—no fuel," says Robo Joe. "But here's a question: Do you want a boy car or a girl car?"

Alice scowls at the robot. "Don't be sexist! Anybody can drive any car they want."

That's not what Car-Boy would say, Mickey thinks. But he decides that now isn't the time to bring up her boyfriend.

The robot chuckles—and coughs up more black smoke.

"I didn't mean a car *for* a boy or a girl, I meant a car that *is* a boy or a girl! True, some cars are neither. But take that one over there—that is definitely a boy car."

Alice furrows her brow. "Hey, that's not Sean's car he's talking about, is it?"

Mickey follows his sister's gaze to a yellow muscle car that looks exactly like Car-Boy's Camaro. Except that the front wheels have been replaced by a pair of huge muscular arms. Huge muscular *human* arms.

"Yes and no," says Mickey. "I think it's Sean *and* his car."

"Right you are! Two for the price of one! Yee-haw!" Joe waves his hat in the air. "That's what we're all about at Robo Joe's."

So *Car-Boy* has become a *boy car*?

The bowlegged robo-cowboy walks squeakily over to the big-armed Camaro and raps his steel knuckles on the hood. "Hey, Big Boy, I brought some friends to see you."

The car's engine growls in reply.

"Sean?" Alice calls out nervously.

Another growl. Not especially encouraging, but not an outright denial.

Then the car straightens his arms into a push-up.

Alice stares at the car in disbelief. "It is him!"

We'll know for sure when he starts taking selfies, thinks Mickey.

Snorting with effort, the car pulls himself upward until he is standing on his back wheels. He flexes his arms, one after the other, like a bodybuilder. More specifically like a teenage bodybuilder named Sean. AKA Car-Boy.

"Sean, I don't know if you can see me, but it's Alice. And Mickey's with me."

At the sound of Mickey's name, the car straightens his arms and moves them robotically back and forth.

"What's he doing?" Alice asks, alarmed.

Mickey blushes. "Imitating me. Just like his friend."

At this, the car's engine erupts in what is unmistakably laughter.

"And laughing at me," says Mickey, gritting his teeth.

"Why? I don't get it," says Alice, clearly perturbed.

"It's . . . not really important."

Even in the Anti-World they make fun of me, Mickey thinks. No place is safe.

"Now, that's enough of that!" says Joe, waving a finger at the Camaro.

The Camaro drops to the ground, and the car's doors fly open.

"He wants us to get in!" Alice exclaims, surprised.

"So we don't have to buy the car first?" asks Mickey.

As Shadow predicted, Joe doesn't demand a high price. He seems offended that Mickey has brought up money at all.

"I'm not some greedy auto rustler!" cries the robot. "You think I'm gonna charge you an arm and a leg? All I want is a few fingers and an ear."

Mickey pales. Is he serious? The Camaro isn't the only car in the lot to incorporate a body part or two.

"I'm just yankin' your chain!" Joe laughs loudly, then coughs even more loudly. "The car is yours. Completely free. Now *that's* what you call a deal, am I right?"

"Right you are, Joe," says Shadow. "You're the best dealmaker in town."

Joe tips his hat in acknowledgment, and an odd, secretive look passes between him and Shadow.

Felicity flies right into Shadow's face, buzzing with suspicion.

"What was that look?" she demands. "Is there perhaps another deal being made here? One that we don't know about?"

"Are all flying houses as paranoid as you?" Shadow scoffs, waving her away.

Felicity glares at him with every one of her window-pane eyes, then rises into the air without another word.

"She's a little sensitive," says Mickey uneasily, watching her go.

"Well, you gonna give this guy a spin or what?" Shadow asks, gesturing toward the driver's seat.

But when Mickey opens the door and starts to climb in, the door slams shut, almost catching his foot. "Hey!"

The car honks in a way that sounds distinctly like a jeer.

"Okay, ha-ha, you got me," says Mickey, shaking his head.

He opens the door again. The door slams shut again. The car honks again.

"Cut it out, Sean!" says Alice. "Behave."

Shadow laughs. "I don't think he likes you, Mickey."

"Yeah, well, the feeling's mutual."

Mickey opens the car door once more. This time, Robo Joe intervenes, holding the door with all four of his arms until Mickey is safely tucked inside.

"Shotgun!" says Shadow, swinging himself into the passenger seat.

The interior of the Camaro looks much the way it did at the time Mickey made the car disappear. The only difference he can see is in the dials behind the steering wheel. Although the car is motionless, the speedometer and gas gauge are moving up and down, in rhythm.

"It's like they're measuring his heart rate," says Alice wonderingly from Mickey's shoulder.

A key is stuck in the ignition. Mickey turns it.

The car horn blares angrily.

"I wouldn't touch that," says Joe, leaning into the driver's-side window. "Just put your hands on the wheel and let him do everything else."

Mickey reaches for the wheel—only to hear the horn blare again. Car-Boy is not making this easy.

"Eh, on second thought," says Joe, "maybe just saddle up and keep your hands to yourself."

Coughing again, the robot slaps the side of the car. "Y'all drive safe now!"

The Camaro bucks and rears in response, throwing Mickey backward into his seat.

Then the car's hands start pawing at the ground, and the car's back wheels start rolling forward.

"Woohoo!" Shadow whoops in delight as they tear off in a cloud of dust.

Mickey glances back at the Pee-ew–turned–Perfume Wagon. The hood seems to be nodding goodbye.

"You don't think Mom's trapped in there, do you?" asks Alice. "The way Sean is?"

"No," says Mickey, with more confidence than he feels. "If she was, she wouldn't let us leave her there. She hates car dealers."

"True. And cowboys."

The two siblings watch silently as their mother's car becomes tinier and tinier behind them.

"Hey, Shadow," says Alice. "You really think the Bubble Gum King can make me big?"

"Yup," says the see-through boy sitting next to them.

"And"—her voice catches—"help us find our parents?"

"Yup again!"

Meanwhile, high above the Camaro, Felicity makes wide arcs in the air, like a police helicopter circling a crime scene.

28.

M is for *mad*.

As a boy, Car-Boy was a jerk who made fun of Mickey. As a car, Car-Boy is still a jerk who makes fun of Mickey.

What's more, he's jerk-*y*.

The car jerks up and down, and back and forth, as if there were big bumps or deep potholes all over the road. (There aren't.) Mickey suspects he's being jerked around intentionally, but he can't be sure. He's never been in an arm-powered car before. Maybe Car-Boy is incapable of a smooth ride, given the way he has to pull himself along with his hands.

As for Mickey's hands, after some initial grumbling, Car-Boy has allowed Mickey to rest them on the steering wheel, but he made it clear that Mickey is not to steer.

If Mickey wants him to turn, Mickey is to ask. In words. And then Car-Boy might or might not comply.

"At least the dude can move," says Shadow, as if

hearing Mickey's thoughts. "Those are some serious guns."

Mickey looks blankly at Shadow.

"You know, arm muscles? Biceps?"

"Yeah, he's pretty proud of those," Mickey grumbles. "You should see his Instagram."

They have been driving for over twenty minutes with no air-conditioning—Car-Boy started blasting the heat when Mickey asked for cold air—and Mickey is not feeling very well.

In the distance, purple mountains loom—among them, hopefully, Bubble Mountain. But they look no closer than they did from Robo Joe's.

Mickey is convinced this ride will never end.

"Why does it feel like we're going in circles?" asks Alice.

No longer on Mickey's shoulder, she has been sitting in a cup holder attached to the dashboard—her very own balcony seat.

"Because we are," says Shadow. "The Anti-World is shaped like a circle."

Mickey looks out his window—the arroyo is still on his left. He checks his compass—they're still headed toward *M*. As far as he can tell, they've been going in a straight line.

And yet he has the same feeling Alice does. He keeps expecting to see his school.

"Well, actually," says Shadow, "it's more like a spiral."

"A spiral?" echoes Alice.

"Yeah, you go around and around, but each time on a different level? No, wait . . . What do you call a circle, or like a ribbon, that twists around like this?" Shadow demonstrates with his hands.

"A Möbius strip?" suggests Mickey.

"Dude! That's it! The Anti-World is a Möbius strip." Shadow scratches his head. "Or maybe not."

"Just so long as you're sure we're going the right way," says Mickey, getting worried.

"Sure, I'm sure," says Shadow. "I know the way to Bubble Mountain like I know the back of your hand."

"You mean the back of *your* hand."

"That's what I said."

"No, it's not," insists Mickey.

The car's engine whines in response, mimicking Mickey's tone if not his words.

Alice giggles.

Mickey glowers.

"You let your boyfriend bully me in the real world and now you're letting him bully me in the Anti-World."

"Oh, come on, that wasn't bullying," says Alice. "It was barely even teasing."

"Only because he can't walk or talk. You know what he said to me the last time I saw him?"

"What?" Alice looks expectantly at Mickey, her little hands resting on the edge of the cup holder.

Mickey hesitates, feeling sweaty.

What was it Car-Boy said exactly? He can't remember.

"It was about bubble gum . . ." he says.

Stalling, Mickey lowers the driver's-side window and faces the wind.

Around them, the red, rocky desert is crowded with cactuses. So far, no cactus has thrown anything at them or even given them the finger. But it is only a matter of time, thinks Mickey.

"You have to admit, you do chew a lot of gum," says Alice.

"See, you're already taking his side!"

Before Alice can respond, Felicity flies in through the open window and hovers between them.

"Mad—it's never more than one argument away," she intones solemnly.

"Oh, you should hear us when we really argue." Alice laughs in the knowing way that usually annoys Mickey, but for once he agrees with her.

"She's right. Some of our arguments are epic."

"No, no, you misunderstand me," says Felicity as she lands gently on the dashboard. "I was just reading that billboard . . ."

Sure enough, several yards ahead, a fiery orange billboard stands on the side of the road:

MAD

It's never more than one argument away!

Farther down the road is another orange billboard:

THIS WAY MADNESS LIES

And even farther down, another:

M is for MAD

"Those signs must be for you, Mickey," says Alice.

"What do you mean?"

"What do you think? That you're mad. All. The. Time." She points up at him from the cup holder.

"Am not!"

His sister looks at him, incredulous.

Mickey blushes.

"Seriously," he says in what he hopes is a more mature tone. "Why does everyone always think I'm mad?"

"Fine, you're never mad," says Alice. "You're the least mad person in the world."

"I mean, I'm not *not* mad . . . Do I have to be anything? Can't I just be nothing?"

"Oh, never mind about that!" Felicity buzzes excitedly. "The point is, we're there. We're *in* Mad. Just like the directions said."

She tilts her wing toward another road sign. It looks like it might mark the entrance to a small town or national park.

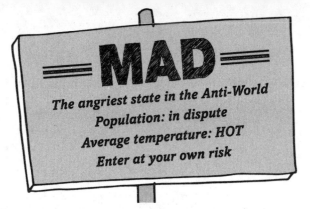

MAD

The angriest state in the Anti-World
Population: in dispute
Average temperature: HOT
Enter at your own risk

Dozens more signs follow, scattered among the rocks and cactuses. They come in a multitude of shapes and sizes and colors, but they all contain variations of the same message.

NOPE!

This is madness!

Don't get even,
GET MAD!

BITE ME

BLEEP!

Yeah right.

Grrr.

I KNOW YOU ARE, BUT WHAT AM I?

Up yours!

YOU WISH.

LOSER! HA . . . *NO.* **WRONG!**

got mad? **YOU SUCK!** NOTHING DOING.

Because you're not worth it.

NOT YOURS, MINE.

JUST SAY NO

Oh no you don't . . . **GET LOST!**

FAIL!!! *i'm hatin' it* *Buzz off.*

NO NO NO NO NO *JUST DON'T DO IT.*

Mickey laughs nervously. "They really want you to get mad in Mad, don't they?"

"It's terrible!" agrees Felicity, who sits squarely in the middle of the Camaro's dashboard, like some sort of navigation device. "Is no one regulating the media environment? How are we to stay positive when we are bombarded by these awful messages?"

Shadow shrugs. "Just try not to let anything tick you off."

"Don't worry, my sister thinks I'm mad all the time, but it's totally not true," says Mickey.

He looks at Alice for a reaction, but she studiously ignores him.

"It's just . . . sometimes I don't want to deal?" Why does he feel the need to explain himself?

"I feel you," says Shadow. "But watch your back. You never know who's going to be lurking behind a corner."

"Like an invisible Anti-Boy, for instance?"

"Ha! Good one." Shadow flashes a smile that may or may not be sincere.

Felicity perks up when they pass another billboard. "Well, that's a much nicer message! Not that I condone vandalism, of course."

The billboard has recently been painted over, and gold graffiti is scrawled across the plain white surface.

THE DOODLER SAYS,
BE A LOVER, NOT A BITER!

"Do you suppose there's someone around here who has a problem with biting?" reflects Felicity. "A toddler perhaps? A dog?"

"I have no idea," says Alice. "But Noodle is definitely more of a lover than a biter."

"Who is?" The flyhouse's windowpanes blink in confusion. "Did you say *Doodle*? Like the Doodler?"

"No, *Noodle*. Like . . . our dog. Although he is a doodle, come to think of it. That's how he got his name. Remember, Mickey?"

"Yeah, but we don't need to talk about that," says Mickey, reddening.

"Oh, yes we do!"

Gleefully, Alice tells the story:

When Mickey's family met Noodle at the pet adoption fair, they were told that the then-nameless dog was an "oodle." Possibly a schnoodle (a schnauzer-poodle mix), but most likely a doodle (a retriever-poodle mix), and more specifically a golden doodle (a golden retriever–poodle mix).

Mickey, then only four years old, misheard. "A noodle! He's a golden noodle!" the little boy cried.

The name stuck.

Alas, Mickey quickly discovered that the golden noodle's hairs were not noodles. In fact, they weren't edible at all.

Undaunted, having learned that Noodle was a doodle, not a noodle, Mickey decided he should encourage the dog's artistic instincts. Soon, the entire house was covered in "Noodle doodles," that is, paw prints. The doodles didn't stop until Mickey's parents caught Mickey red-handed, dipping the dog's paws in finger paint and sending the dog skidding across the floor.

"Awww. What an adorable story!" exclaims Felicity. "I wish I'd known you then, Mickey. You must have been such a cutie-pie."

"Anyway . . ." says Mickey, trying to change the subject. "Who's the Doodler?"

"Nobody you want to know," says Shadow darkly. "He's no friend of the king, let's put it that way."

"Why not?"

"You know how kings are. They don't like it when people pop bubbles in their faces."

Mickey feels a sudden rush of anxiety. Does Shadow know about him popping bubbles in his father's class? How could he know about that?

"But don't stress, my dude," Shadow says reassuringly. "BGK is gonna love you!"

"BGK?"

"Yeah. *B-G-K*. Bubble Gum King. That's what his buddies call him. Or sometimes the Bubblicious BGK. Or His Bubbleness. Or the Bubbly One. Or the Big Bubbly. Or Bubble Trouble . . . He loves it when you tease him like that. Usually. But you gotta watch out. Like, you'll just be hanging, and he'll be all laughing like you're his best bud, then suddenly—" Shadow draws his finger across his throat. "What!!! Just fooling!"

"You sure?" Mickey's mouth feels dry.

"Yeah. But, hey, if you're worried, you can, I dunno, bring him a gift. Everyone likes a gift, right?"

Mickey nods, pale.

He has been so eager to get to Bubble Mountain that he almost forgot about the trials that will face him when he gets there.

The contest he must win. The king he must win over.

29.

Go mad.

They are definitely going in circles. Mickey can tell by the building that lies straight ahead.

Alice sees it too. "Desert Donut! Can we go in? I'm dying for a Cactuccino."

"What are you going to do, soak in it?" asks Mickey. "A cup would be like a bathtub for you. Besides, it's completely dark. Or not—"

As he speaks, the shop's interior lights up. The shop's exterior lights up too—with a new name.

"*Desert Health-Nut*," says Alice. "Is that a joke?"

A new menu is painted on the window.

Mickey leans out of the Camaro and reads with distaste. "*Whole-wheat donut holes . . . Beet shakes . . .* Sorry, no Cactuccinos!"

"Mom would be all over those beet shakes," says Alice. "But yeah, not for me. Let's keep going."

As if out of nowhere, gray clouds have started to cluster in the sky, casting shadows over the landscape.

Weather changes fast in the desert; apparently it changes fast in the Anti-Desert too.

The street looks very gloomy. But as they drive by, businesses light up, one by one.

Next is a clothing store.

ITCHY RICHIE'S TOO BIG OR TOO SMALL
Where nothing fits quite right,
and all the underwear is too loose or too tight!

Mickey thinks back to his list. He remembers writing *tight underwear* in the Anti-Book. Also *loose underwear*. Now the only kind of underwear *not* available is the kind that fits.

"Who buys this stuff?" asks his sister, aghast.

"Nobody?" Mickey glances around. Although businesses appear to be opening, the street remains completely quiet.

Once, Mickey went on a tour of a movie studio in Los Angeles. He walked down a street where all the storefronts were just that. Fronts. With no backs.

He has the feeling that these stores are like those. Empty shells. Fakes.

"Why isn't anybody here?" he asks.

"We're here, aren't we?" Shadow answers.

"Yeah, but it's like a ghost town. Where are all the other people?"

"Like who? You're the guy with the Anti-Book."

"What does the Anti-Book have to do with it?" asks Alice.

"Only everything," says Shadow, as if the answer were obvious.

Disconcerted, Mickey asks Car-Boy to pull over in front of a store called THAT'S NOT A TOY! TOYS & GIFTS.

"Maybe I can find a present for the king in there."

"Maybe," says Shadow, not very encouragingly. "I think I'll wait outside. I like my toys to be toys."

"And I think I'll just have a quick fly-around," says Felicity. "Don't listen to him, Mickey. I'm sure the king will appreciate anything you find. I know I would."

With Alice on his shoulder, Mickey cautiously opens the door to the toy store. Far from empty, it is chock-full of merchandise, divided into three aisles:

BATTERIES INCLUDED	ALREADY OPEN	NEVER BREAKS

Exactly like Mickey specified in the Anti-Book. Or rather, exactly *not* like.

Mickey knows this would be a good time to tell Alice about the book, but he can't make himself do it. He keeps thinking about how mad she'll be.

"Well, I guess it's better than dividing them by boy toys and girl toys, like Robo Joe and his cars," says Alice. "Do you know they even make girl blocks now? Like a girl will only want to build something if it's pink and sparkly. It's so gross."

"Tell that to your boyfriend."

"What do you mean?"

"Nothing . . . You don't think the king wants batteries, do you?"

The BATTERIES INCLUDED aisle includes no toys, only batteries. Thousands and thousands of batteries. Some new. Some corroded. Some sparking dangerously.

"I'm guessing kings have plenty of batteries," says Alice.

Bypassing the batteries, Mickey proceeds down the ALREADY OPEN aisle. Here at least the toys are intact. It is the packaging that is missing. Or in some cases, lying in shreds on the floor, as if left there by a young child after a meltdown.

"Just tell me what Sean said already," says Alice. "You obviously want to. You keep bringing it up."

"It's just that he thinks gum is girly or . . . or something," says Mickey, stumbling on the words. "Maybe because it's pink. I dunno."

He knows he's leaving something out. Something Car-Boy said that was even more irksome. More irritating. More utterly infuriating. But he still can't remember what it is.

"It's stupid," he says. "Forget I mentioned it."

"Okay."

Mickey looks at his little big sister suspiciously. "So you're not going to defend him?"

"About that? No. If he really said gum is girly, you're right, it's totally stupid."

Mickey nods, grateful. And surprised.

He stops at a shelf loaded with dolls—more precisely, with multiple versions of the same famous blond doll. Having lost their packaging, the dolls lie in disarray, clothes strewn around them.

"Speaking of girly, most of those outfits would almost fit you," says Mickey. "Just think—you can be a flight attendant or a doctor or a disco dancer . . ."

He holds up the disco dancer doll to show his sister. It is just a bit taller than she is.

She glares at him. "I'm not a doll."

"I was just joking. Sheesh." Mickey puts the doll back. "Anyway, you used to love to play dress-up with me, remember? You never had a problem making *me* into a doll."

"You were four years old."

"And then six . . . and then eight . . ."

"Okay, I wouldn't mind wearing that hat." Alice points to a doll in a cowboy hat and boots. "But only if you put on that tutu we passed."

Mickey makes a face. "Really?"

"You loved tutus when you were little," says Alice. "You wore them on your head."

"Did not."

"You so did."

"Okay, it's a deal," says Mickey, handing her the cowboy hat she requested. "You wear the hat, I wear the tutu."

"And one of those horns," says his sister, pointing to a rack of headbands with unicorn horns and cat ears. "They're just like the one you used to have."

"No way! No unicorns!" says Mickey. "The deal is off."

"Why? You used to be obsessed with unicorns."

"Only because you wouldn't let me like Pegasuses. You got all the flying horses. I got the horses with one horn and no powers."

"Yeah, because I was worried you'd go flying off a table again if you played Pegasus! Besides, you have to admit, unicorns are way cooler."

"They're embarrassing."

"Why? Oh!" says Alice, reading his face. "You're talking about Dad's class, aren't you?"

She smiles knowingly. "The Gender Unicorn. That's the worst. I'm so sorry that you had to go through that . . . No, I'm not sorry. I had to too. So it's only fair."

"Did Dad tell everyone in your class that *you* went through a unicorn phase?" says Mickey. "I don't think so."

Alice winces in sympathy. "Ooh. That's rough. You win."

"Everybody kept looking at me like they felt really sorry for me, but also like they wanted to roll on the floor laughing."

"That sounds about right."

"Gee, thanks."

Conveniently forgetting the unicorn horn and the tutu, Mickey leaves the ALREADY OPEN aisle, and starts walking down the NEVER BREAKS aisle. Rather than toys, the shelves here are stocked with rocks and steel bars and blocks of cement.

"The king might need cement," jokes Alice. "For building a castle or whatever."

Mickey picks up a small piece, pretending to ponder the idea. "No, too heavy to carry," he says, putting it down.

"Hey, do you remember that summer you dyed my hair a different color every day for a week?" he asks.

"And then dyed the dog to match? Uh-huh," says Alice, smiling. "By the time school started, your hair was a total mess. But Noodle's tail was a perfect rainbow."

"Dad wasn't too happy about that."

"Mom thought it was hysterical. Especially when we put your unicorn horn on him."

"Maybe that's why they got a divorce," says Mickey. "It was all about the rainbow dog tail."

They both laugh. It's the first time they've laughed together in months, maybe since their parents separated.

"Hey, do you think there's any food in the Anti-World?" asks Alice. "Besides beet shakes, I mean. I'm starving— aren't you?"

"I just want some gum," Mickey admits.

"You guys coming or what?" Shadow shouts from outside.

"I guess I'm not going to find a present in here," says Mickey.

"Let's just get to Bubble Mountain," says Alice as they

head toward the exit. "Then you can have as much gum as you want, and we can go back to normal life, okay?"

Donning her headphones, Alice slides down from Mickey's neck into the hood of his sweatshirt.

Normal like when he was little? Mickey wants to ask. Or normal like yesterday?

The first seems more fun. Even if it means wearing a unicorn horn again.

30.

Cop-*y* like cop-*ish*.

When he gets outside, Mickey nearly bumps into Shadow. The almost-invisible boy puts his finger to his lips and gestures for Mickey to remain still.

Across the street, two figures in police uniforms are walking by—on all fours.

"Best to stay out of their way," whispers Shadow.

Alice peers over Mickey's shoulder.

"Are those cops or cats?" she asks.

"Both," Shadow says. "They're Copy Cats."

"Isn't that what you call those cats next door, Mickey?" asks Alice. "The ones that are always copying each other?"

"And always stealing food from the neighbors," says Mickey. "Yeah."

"So these are the anti-versions?"

"I guess?"

"You've got it all wrong, dudes." Shadow shakes his

head. "It's not copy, like make a copy. It's cop-*y*, like cop-*ish* or cop-*esque* or cop-*like*. They're like cops, but not quite, because, hello!, they're cats."

Mickey looks again. If you ignore the uniforms, there is no doubt the cats across the street resemble the thieving tabbies.

They may be cops now, but they were once robbers.

After the cats disappear around the corner, Mickey follows Shadow back toward the Camaro.

"Hey, look out—" Mickey's sister tugs on his ear.

"Ow!" He pushes away her tiny hand with his finger. "What?"

"Too late!" says Alice, annoyed. "You already stepped in it." Mickey looks down. Something glitters at his feet.

Shadow laughs. "Oops!"

Holding her nose, Alice retreats into his hood.

"Yuck," complains Mickey. "More gold poop."

"Wait!" says Felicity, appearing above their heads. "Don't waste it!"

The flyhouse swoops in as Mickey wipes the bottom of his shoe on the curb. He's making a stinky sandy mess.

"Oh, no! It's all mixed together!" Distressed, Felicity starts picking grains of sand out of the soft wet pile. "How am I going to get a good clean bite?"

"You wouldn't know it, but this is her third poop of the day!" says Mickey.

Shadow smirks. "Three square meals, huh?"

"Tastes differ," says Felicity, glowering at them with

every one of her windowpane eyes. "It is ignorant as well as unkind to judge the eating habits of others."

With a sniff, she returns to her task.

"Look, the cats came back," says Alice, peeking out of Mickey's hood.

Farther down the block, the Copy Cats are standing on their hind legs.

In front of them is a cement wall, decorated with more of the Doodler's gold graffiti.

THE DOODLER SAYS, STAND BY YOUR PACK

Scowling and hissing, one cat gestures angrily at the wall while the other unrolls a big poster.

Then the cats lick their paws and smooth the poster over the graffiti, covering it entirely.

Mickey can just make out the words.

WANTED:
DEAD OR ALIVE!
THE VILE ANTI-VILLAIN KNOWN AS
THE DOODLER
SAVE THE ANTI-KINGDOM
FROM THIS TERRIBLE MENACE
WARNING: HE IS LEGGED AND DANGEROUS
BIG REWARD!
BY ORDER OF HIS ROYAL MAJESTY
THE BUBBLE GUM KING

"Legged and dangerous?" Felicity buzzes nervously. "I wonder how many legs he has. Must be a lot to make him so dangerous. Dozens, I suppose. Flies have only six legs, of course. And houses . . . well, I think we know I'm not a villain!"

"Isn't it supposed to be *armed* and dangerous?" asks Alice.

"What do you know about this guy?" Mickey asks Shadow, frowning. "He doesn't have anything to do with me, does he?"

"No!" says Shadow sharply. "Why would you think that?"

"Well, he's an anti-villain and you said I was the anti-hero . . ."

"So?" says Shadow, only slightly less sharply. "I told you, everyone around here is an anti-something or other."

Mickey looks searchingly at him. There's no doubt Shadow is acting strangely. He seems uncomfortable being so close to the Copy Cats.

Suddenly, Mickey remembers Mime-Boy's warning. *Beware shh-*blank.

Beware Shadow.

"It's not you, is it?" Mickey asks in as casual a tone as he can muster. "You're not the Doodler . . . ?"

"Nobody can even see me! How could I be on a wanted poster?"

"It's not like there's a picture."

"Trust me," says Shadow. "I'm not the Doodler."

"Okay, okay. Sorry!"

What a dumb thing to ask, thinks Mickey, embarrassed. Shadow wouldn't confess to being a criminal any more than Mickey would tell Alice about the Anti-Book.

Finished with the poster, the Copy Cats drop onto all fours. They look hard at Mickey, then slip quietly away, as if tailing a suspect.

Mickey shudders. Those cats give him the creeps.

"C'mon, Felicity," he says.

The flyhouse, still absorbed in her golden meal, glances up at Mickey with one of her many eyes. "You go. Unlike you, I have no need of wheels. Besides, I smell another pile of gold downwind. I may go that way first."

Alice giggles. "You're saying you want to follow the poop?"

"Why not?" responds the flyhouse stiffly. "That's a charming idea. A trail of golden poo—it's like something out of a fairy tale."

"You're going to leave us?" Mickey is taken aback. He's gotten used to having her around, almost as if she really were his house.

"You'll be fine. You have another guide now."

She looks with undisguised disdain in Shadow's direction.

"I'll catch up later. Who knows, maybe I'll learn something useful in the meantime."

Learn something about Shadow, she seems to be saying.

"Okay, then goodbye, I guess," Mickey says grudgingly.

Shadow looks down at Mickey's foot. "Better make sure that shoe is clean. Car-Boy might not like having poop smeared all over his floor mats."

"I should leave it just to get him back," says Mickey.

But he wipes the last bits of poop off of his shoe anyway.

Shadow just called Sean "Car-Boy," Mickey thinks. How does Shadow know that name?

"You can read my thoughts, can't you?" Mickey asks.

"Me?" Shadow seems amused, but he doesn't deny it. "I'm the invisible guy. You should look into mine."

Mickey walks around Shadow, examining him. "You know, you're not that invisible anymore."

"Cool," says Shadow. "We must be getting closer."

"To where?"

"Our destination."

Without explaining further, he gets into the car.

31.

Screeeeeeech!

Screeeeeech! Car-Boy hits the brakes.

"Hey, careful! There's no seat belt in here," shouts Alice, bracing herself against the side of the cup holder.

Mickey, who *is* wearing a seat belt, nonetheless lurches forward, almost hitting the windshield with his forehead.

He blinks in surprise.

"What is it?" asks Alice. "I can't see from here!"

"I don't know. I'm hallucinating. I must be hungry after all."

"Why? What are you seeing?"

"Um, cookies, I think? Two huge chocolate chip cookies."

As the two round objects come closer, he sees that he was right. Both cookies are about five feet in diameter and dotted with chocolate, but their postures could not be more different. One cookie is ramrod stiff, and hopping toward them with almost military precision. The other cookie is quite wiggly, bending this way and that as it rolls down the road.

"Greetings, travelers!" says the wiggly cookie. "Do you have room for two yummy home-baked cookies? We're not going far."

The cookies peer into Mickey's open window, and their chocolate chip eyes light up.

"Mickey, what a coincidence!" exclaims the stiff cookie. "We were just talking about you."

Mickey recognizes their voices immediately. It's Crispy Charlie and Chewy Charlie. Transformed into giant dessert items.

So *Chocolate Chip Charlies* have become what? *Charlie Chip Cookies?*

What did Shadow say about the negative of a negative . . . ?

The logic of the Anti-Book is not very logical.

"Come out so we can get a look at you," says Crispy Charlie. "Don't be shy."

As Mickey climbs out of the car, Chewy Charlie eyes him with concern. "How are you, Mickey? You look like you're carrying a lot of tension in your shoulders."

"I'm fine," says Mickey uncomfortably.

Shadow gets out from the other side of the car and watches with a wry expression on his face.

"You haven't been keeping up with your practice, have you?" Chewy Charlie persists.

By practice, she means yoga practice. She has been

trying to get Mickey to do yoga for the better part of a year.

"Well, no time like the present," she declares. "I could use a good stretch myself."

Before Mickey can answer, the yoga-instructor–turned–chocolate-chip-cookie bends over.

"Let's start with Downward Dog. Hold for two breaths . . . Plank pose. Then Cobra. Chest up. Breathe . . ."

Without looking at Mickey, who has not moved an inch, the ultra-flexible cookie flips onto her back and performs another series of yoga poses.

"Now Bridge into Wheel."

Behind her, Shadow mimics her motions. Mickey chokes back a laugh.

"Enough!" scolds Crispy Charlie. "Can't you see that he doesn't want to do yoga? Mickey, are you hungry? Can I tempt you with a bite?"

She turns her side to him, as if she is offering her shoulder to nibble on.

"No, I'm good," says Mickey quickly.

Now that he's out of the car, he realizes that he's very hungry indeed. But hungry enough to eat his soon-to-be stepmother? No.

"Oh, just take one. I'm told my cookies are so delicious, they should be illegal." Crispy Charlie laughs, putting something in his hand. "Ironic, considering I'm a lawyer!"

For a second, Mickey fears that it is her hand itself that she has handed to him. But when he looks down, he is relieved to see a normal cookie.

"They should be illegal with all that sugar!" says Chewy Charlie, handing one of her own cookies to Mickey. "Me, I'm sweetened with agave syrup. Much healthier."

"Cookies aren't supposed to be healthy!" retorts Crispy Charlie.

"Ask them if they've seen our parents," Alice shouts from the cup holder.

"Alice, is that you? You look so cute in that size!" says Chewy Charlie. "Sorry, we've been on our own ever since this wonderful metamorphosis took hold of us."

"In fact, we're looking for your parents now," says Crispy Charlie. "But here, have a cookie!"

She tosses a cookie into the cup holder, where it lands at Alice's feet. It's almost as big as Alice is.

"Okay, well, bye," says Mickey. He is in a hurry to end the conversation before his stepmothers ask for a ride again.

He ducks back into the car, placing his two cookies on the dashboard. Shadow slides in on the other side.

Chewy Charlie looks startled.

"That's it?" she asks, stopping Mickey from closing the car door. "Not even a hug? We're family."

Mickey avoids her eyes. "Not yet," he says, unable to hide the bitterness in his voice.

"Oh, come on, Mickey," says Crispy Charlie. "Your parents broke up. It happens."

"You can't control everything," says Chewy Charlie philosophically. "Sometimes, you just have to say, Well, that's the way the cookie crumbles."

"What a dumb expression," Shadow whispers from the passenger seat. "A cookie doesn't just crumble—someone has to crumble it."

He's right, Mickey thinks.

"A cookie doesn't just crumble by itself," he repeats loudly. "And neither did my family! You crumbled it. Both of you."

Mickey slams the car door shut. Everyone stares at him.

"I must say, I'm a little surprised to hear you talk this way," says Crispy Charlie through the open window. "Didn't you tell me you wanted to be emancipated from your parents?"

Mickey grunts noncommittally. He is as shocked as everyone else by his outburst.

"Usually, you have to be at least sixteen, but there are exceptions," she persists. "It would be a conflict of interest for me to represent you, but I can refer you to a good lawyer."

"See, you want me to leave!" snaps Mickey. "I knew all those cookies you baked were a fake-out."

Shadow leans over Mickey and shouts out the window. "Why don't you two leave him alone and go marry each other instead?"

Mickey stares at him in guilty surprise. Those exact words had been in Mickey's head for nearly a year, but he'd kept them to himself.

The cookies eye each other and shake their heads.

"Sorry, she's just not my type of cookie," says Chewy Charlie. "I'm vegan. She's made with butter. Now, a peanut butter cookie, that might be different."

"You really go for those nutty types, don't you?" quips Crispy Charlie.

"Or a nice glass of oat milk perhaps . . ."

As Chewy Charlie continues to muse about possible romantic partners, Crispy Charlie turns back to Mickey. "Please don't blame us for your parents' choices."

"She's right," says Alice. "If you're going to be mad at anyone, be mad at Mom and Dad."

"For the last time, I'M NOT MAD!!!"

Mickey brings his fist down hard on the dashboard, sending his two cookies skidding into the windshield. The Camaro's horn blares in response.

"What?" says Mickey fiercely to the car. "You want me to do that again?"

He raises his fist.

Everyone stares at him.

"Okay, so . . . m-maybe that was a little . . ." Mickey stammers, uncurling his fist.

"But that doesn't mean . . ." He trails off.

He can feel his heart beating in his chest and there is an uncomfortable prickling sensation in his face.

"Anyway, um, sorry for what I said." He takes a breath. "My sister's right. It's not your fault. It's our parents'."

"Apology accepted," says Crispy Charlie.

"Let's go," says Chewy Charlie. "He needs space to process. Mickey, we're here for you when you need us."

Nodding their goodbyes, the cookies hop and roll out of sight.

32.

Boom!

"So, basically, you're saying I'm a total raging maniac and everybody knows it except me," says Mickey when they're moving again.

He looks at Alice, daring her to contradict him. "Well?" As long as they're talking about it, he wants to hear the worst.

"Let's just say you yell a lot—especially at Mom," says Alice, who is bracing herself against the side of the cup holder as Car-Boy barrels toward Bubble Mountain. "And you barely even speak to Dad. You've been giving him the silent treatment for like a year."

"See, you always take everybody else's side."

"Just because I talk to them, that doesn't mean I'm not mad about it too. I mean, we didn't do anything to deserve it, did we?"

"Yeah, no, but . . ."

"But what? Our parents are getting divorced! We're *supposed* to be mad. It would be weird if we weren't."

Sitting in the passenger seat, Shadow nods in agreement. "Well, you're pretty weird either way," he qualifies, "but she's got a point."

"I thought you told me not to get mad. And now what? You want me to start ranting?"

"Start?" says Shadow.

Mickey glares at him.

"Chillax, dude. I was just agreeing in general, not that you should be mad right this second."

Mickey looks out the window and watches the desert speed by. To the left are the red, rocky foothills. Ahead are the dark, foreboding mountains.

He could be looking at a picture of his mind.

He, Mickey, *is* mad. At everyone. But mostly at his parents.

Why did he not admit this before? It just seemed so childish. Or uncool. Or something. Lots of people get divorced, he thought. Why should his parents be different? And why should their divorce concern him anyway?

But it does concern him. Clearly.

His parents are *his* parents. Their divorce is *his* divorce.

They not only abandoned each other when they split up, they also abandoned their family. They abandoned *him*.

And it wasn't just his dad who left. His mom left too.

At least, that's how it felt. With her leaving every morning to get to Chewy Charlie's yoga class. And always being late when she was supposed to pick up Mickey after school. And then there were those online business courses she started taking at night. What happened to the no-screens-at-dinner rule, anyway?

Sure, Mickey might have told his parents to get lost a few times. Or more than a few times. But only because *he'd* already lost *them*.

It's like when someone says, "I hate you!" and you say, "I hate you first!" It's not necessarily true; you're just trying to save face.

"I guess I am mad . . . a little. Okay, a lot."

Mickey flushes with embarrassment. But also with relief. How could he have not seen it when everyone else did?

"It's so selfish when you think about it," he says to his sister. "Couldn't they at least wait until we were in college?"

Alice shrugs unhappily. She doesn't have an answer.

Shadow nods in sympathy. "Yeah, like, do they really love those . . . cookies more than they love you?"

Mickey narrows his eyes. "Are you *trying* to make us feel bad?"

There is a faint BOOM in the distance. Thunder perhaps.

"It's almost like they never loved you," Shadow continues. "Like, maybe love doesn't even exist."

"Wow," says Alice. "That's pretty harsh."

"Yeah . . . pretty . . . harsh," says Mickey, feeling suddenly like he's choking.

Shadow is speaking Mickey's thoughts aloud again. But this time they're thoughts he never knew he had.

"Sorry, dudes, just calling it like I see it," says Shadow.

"Sure, that's what *this* guy always says." Mickey points at the steering wheel.

The car's engine whines in imitation of Mickey's tone.

There is another BOOM in the distance.

Alice frowns. "Sean, if you make fun of my little brother again, or talk any more smack about the way he chews gum, or mess with him in any way at all, I'm going to hurt you." She pokes the dashboard. "Got it?"

Mickey looks away. Coming from someone her size, her threats may not carry much weight, but he appreciates her protective, big-sisterly impulse.

And he doesn't want her to see the tears welling in his eyes.

The car rumbles in response, but in a less threatening manner than before. Who knows—maybe Alice got through to him.

Another BOOM. Slightly louder this time.

Mickey glances out the window but sees nothing amiss. Or nothing that wasn't already amiss.

Alice looks at the abandoned cookie lying by her feet. "I thought I was over these, but I'm *so* hungry . . ."

She lifts the edge of the cookie. It's heavy but not too heavy.

Mickey picks up one of his cookies off the dashboard. "Me too. I thought the Charlies ruined them forever."

"I know, right?" says Shadow. "What did they think? They could buy you off with cookies?" He grins conspiratorially at Mickey.

Mickey does not grin back. He is growing very tired of Shadow speaking his mind for him.

"Down with chocolate chip cookies!" declares Shadow, undeterred. "Let's toss 'em out the window!"

He reaches for Alice's cookie, but she waves him away.

"Actually, I was just about to eat this." Alice raises the cookie to her mouth and nibbles at an exposed chocolate chip. For her, the chip is the size of a candy bar. "I forgot how much I loved these cookies."

"Yeah, me too," says Mickey. He bites into Crispy Charlie's cookie, trying not to think about her shoulder. "And to tell the truth, the only reason they started baking cookies is because I asked them to."

"Okay, be like that," complains Shadow. "Next thing you'll be calling them Mom One and Mom Two. Or is it Mom Two and Mom Three? One big happy mommy family."

"You know, that's kind of offensive," says Mickey.

"Kind of?" says Alice.

"Okay, more than kind of."

If Shadow isn't the Anti-Villain, maybe he's something worse, Mickey thinks. And harder to escape.

BOOM!

The sound is much louder now.

BOOM!

Louder still.

Mickey's second cookie slides off the dashboard.

BOOM!

This time the sound is deafening. Whatever is making it is not far away.

Alice stands on tiptoe, trying to see out the rear window. "Mickey, can you see anything?"

Mickey shakes his head. "Sounds like something big, though."

Alice points at Shadow. "Do you know what's happening?"

"Nope," says Shadow, seemingly unfazed.

"So invisible people don't have X-ray vision or supersonic hearing or anything?"

"Not usually."

CRASH! BOOM! CRASH!

The ground shakes as if an earthquake is in progress.

Felicity flies in through the driver's-side window, buzzing frantically. "Thank goodness I found you!"

"Felicity, you're back!" Mickey exclaims. He is delighted to see her, but he can tell she's upset. "Did you, um, find anything out?"

He means, *Did you find anything out about Shadow?*

"Yes! That's why I'm here. It's the Mad Dam—it burst open. There's a tsunami headed this way!"

"A tsunami?!" Alice yelps. "Well, we better not just sit here. Sean, move!"

"I think he's going as fast as he can," says Mickey.

Car-Boy revs his motor, as if to say, *Oh yeah?*

He accelerates, slamming Mickey into the back of his seat and almost knocking Alice out of the cup holder.

In a second, he's going so fast, his arms are a blur. So fast, they look more like propellers than arms.

But it's not fast enough.

Mickey looks out the back window. "Uh-oh . . ."

"What? What is it?" asks Alice.

"Water." He grips the steering wheel tight in his hands. "A lot of it."

The car's engine screams in unmistakable panic.

"Mickey, I just remembered," says Alice. "Sean can't swim! He's scared of water."

"That's . . . not good," says Mickey, over the sound of rushing water.

He is disturbed—and just a little bit gratified—to hear that Car-Boy has this unexpected weakness.

"Doesn't matter," says Shadow. "Nobody could swim in that anyway."

Suddenly, an enormous wave crashes over them. They are submerged.

Felicity stares at the murky, swirling water as she struggles to stay aloft. "I just learned something about myself," she says. "I'm scared of water too."

"Mickey, do something!" Alice screams.

Mickey's eyes are wide in the darkness. "What do I do?"

"I don't know—roll down the window! Isn't that what you're supposed to do? So we can swim out?"

Mickey reaches for the window, but is thrown back as the car tumbles deeper.

"Easy, kids. Nobody's drowning yet." Shadow pats Mickey on the shoulder. "Just chill for a sec."

As Mickey attempts to chill, the car does a somersault.

Then, in a flurry of bubbles, they are tossed violently upward until they fly clear out of the water.

The car almost flips over before crashing back into the river below.

Nobody says a word. They can't catch their breath long enough.

Mickey expects to sink again, but instead they bob up and down in the turbulent water. Mickey's head is jerked back and forth, but at least, he notes, he's breathing.

"Oh, thank goodness, we're alive!" exclaims Felicity. "I couldn't live with myself if we died."

"No, you probably couldn't," says Shadow sardonically.

Soon they are spinning in the current like an out-of-control canoe. Sean's arms flap up and down furiously—and uselessly—as the car careens every which way.

"What's happening?" asks Alice. "I can't look."

"Um, we're river rafting, kinda," says Mickey.

The river is tar-black. But, in places, it glows orange, like lava. In other places, it glows green, as though infected with some radioactive material.

Bubbles churn the surface, releasing steam into the air.

"What river is this?" Felicity asks. "The Tigris? The Nile? The River Styx? It looks very toxic."

"It's not really a river," says Shadow. "It's anger. Mixed with hate. Maybe some despair."

"Don't tell me that's *my* anger," says Mickey, aghast.

"You poor boy!" exclaims Felicity. "It must have given you terrible indigestion!"

Their conversation is interrupted by the sight of a road sign, half-buried in water:

NOW LEAVING MAD
Remember, what happens in Mad stays mad.

Instinctively, Mickey glances at his compass. No longer pointing to *M,* it's spinning wildly.

part four:

bad

33.

Wrong way!

The river of anger has calmed down. Sort of.

And Car-Boy, the muscle-boy–turned–muscle-car–turned–muscle-boat, is learning to swim. Sort of.

Arms flailing, he splashes in all directions, but at least he is pointing forward.

With Mickey's help, Alice has climbed atop the rear-view mirror, where she has a much better view of their surroundings.

"You're supposed to be making circles with your arms," she directs Car-Boy. "And cup your hands more. That's how you create resistance."

The car's engine sputters noisily. Car-Boy dislikes being told what to do.

"I know what I'm talking about. I was on the swim team, remember?"

"On the bright side, we're not sinking," notes Felicity,

who keeps hovering in front of the steering wheel, much to Mickey's annoyance. "Either this car is more buoyant than it looks, or your anger has been distilled into some thick liquid, dense enough to keep the car afloat."

The car's engine revs with an upward lilt. Car-Boy has a question.

"He wants to know which way to go," says Alice.

Ahead, road signs stick out of the anger-water, pointing in various directions.

THIS WAY

THAT WAY

RIGHT WAY

WRONG WAY

NO WAY

GO AWAY   WAY TO GO

"Not very helpful, are they, those signs?" Felicity buzzes. "I suppose we should choose RIGHT WAY?"

"But we're supposed to go the wrong way," says Mickey. "We get to Bubble Mountain by making a wrong turn, remember?"

His sister raises a tiny eyebrow. "You're saying RIGHT WAY is the wrong way and WRONG WAY is the right way?"

"Right. I mean yes."

"But if WRONG WAY is the right way, then that makes it the wrong way again," Alice points out.

The flyhouse's many windowpanes regard her with skepticism. "So you think RIGHT WAY is the right way and WRONG WAY is the wrong way?"

Alice nods, not very confidently.

"Okay, then I guess we go RIGHT WAY?" Mickey studies the signs yet again, but they offer no more clues.

"Don't be so sure," cautions Felicity. "Because if WRONG WAY is the wrong way, then it's the right way after all, isn't it?"

The car engine groans with frustration and makes a sound that clearly means *Make up your minds already!*

"The directions say to take a wrong turn," says Mickey, who is beginning to get very frustrated himself. "Let's just go with WRONG WAY."

Mickey looks at Shadow for confirmation. "Er, right?"

Shadow laughs. "Do I understand a word you're saying? You guys couldn't tell your left foot from your right butt cheek. What!!!"

Mickey doesn't smile. "You said you knew the way to Bubble Mountain like the back of your hand."

"I do, man, I do!" Shadow shifts in his seat. "But you gotta find your *own* way to Bad—otherwise you never get there. It's a you-do-you kind of thing. You feel me?"

"Sure. Except that you're not making any sense." Exasperated, Mickey puts his head in his hands.

His red compass is lying across his thigh. He notices that the needle has stopped spinning.

"Hey, guys. I think the compass wants us to go to the right. That's the way *B* is. You know, *B* for *Bad* . . . ?"

Car-Boy seems to think that this is the final word, because he abruptly veers to the right. Anger-water sprays in a wide arc as if the Camaro were a speedboat carving a turn in the ocean.

"Nice!" Shadow pronounces. "That turn was hella tight!"

They pass a half-submerged gas station, and a pair of yellow arches indicating that somewhere nearby a fast-food restaurant is underwater.

In the distance, the anger-water ends in a curving line beyond which they can see nothing.

As they get closer, Mickey begins to get nervous. "Hey, um, is that a waterfall ahead of us?"

"Yeah, maybe we should go another way," Alice pipes up from the mirror. "Sean, can we stop and turn around?"

Car-Boy doesn't respond. Neither does he stop.

"Sean," says Alice. "Seriously. Stop!"

Car-Boy sputters and raises his arms helplessly. He can't stop. The current is too strong.

"Uh-oh," says Shadow under his breath. "This is going to be good."

"Good?" repeats Alice, incredulous.

"Well, maybe not *good* good. We are trying to get to Bad, after all."

"I knew WRONG WAY was the wrong way," frets Felicity.

"Mickey, put me back in the cup holder," begs Alice. "No, put me back in your pocket. I don't want to see any more."

Mickey almost says, *Oh, so* now *you want to be in my pocket.* But he does as requested. This is not the time for snark.

It looks very much like they are about to head over a cliff.

"Somebody, please, tell me how I can help!" says Felicity desperately.

"You can't," says Mickey tensely. "You should go."

The flyhouse's windowpanes well with tears. "Never!"

"Go!" Mickey shoos her out the open window. "Save yourself."

"No!" She immediately flies back, hitting the window as he begins to close it behind her. "I will go down with the ship!"

"Go!" Mickey shouts. "Please!"

"No!" Felicity shouts back, heroically clinging to the glass. "Mickey, knowing you has been the highlight of my life."

"You've only been alive for a few hours!"

"You are the greatest human I've ever known!"

"I'm practically the only human you've ever known! And trust me, I'm not worth dying for!"

Felicity's wings bend in the wind. She won't be able to hold on for long.

"Yes, you are!" she shouts through the glass. "Besides, I told you, a fly's life is short!"

"Maybe, but some houses live for hundreds of years!"

"True, but . . ." The flyhouse seems stymied by Mickey's last observation. "Anyway, I'm not abandoning you. You may as well let me back in."

"No! Go!"

Mickey clutches the steering wheel as if it's a life preserver. His knuckles whiten.

For once, Sean doesn't complain about the tight grip.

"So what happens in the Anti-World when you . . . die?" Mickey asks Shadow, not sure he wants to know the answer.

Shadow tilts his head to look at Mickey. "Dude, you should see your face. It's like you're in a horror movie."

"This *is* a horror movie! How can you be so relaxed?"

"Can't anybody do anything?!" Alice yells from inside Mickey's sweatshirt pocket.

Too late. The car-turned-boat has reached the edge. Car-Boy's arms frantically spin backward, but inexorably the car begins to tip downward.

Alice buries herself deeper in Mickey's sweatshirt.

Mickey wants to hide as well, but he forces himself to peer through the windshield.

They are at the top of an enormous curtain of water. Far below, the water disappears into a cloud of mist and spray.

It occurs to him that if he dies, he won't have to worry about going home. Which would be a relief. Except at the same instant something else occurs to him: He *wants* to go home. Desperately.

Even if everyone knows what he did. Even if everyone hates him.

Mickey closes his eyes. Then opens them.

The car hasn't moved.

"Why aren't we falling?" he manages to croak out.

"Good question." Shadow considers. "Sorry to disappoint you, dude, but I don't think this is a waterfall."

"Uh, it looks pretty much exactly like a waterfall."

"Yeah, it does."

"But it isn't?"

"Nope."

They sit there on the edge of doom for another moment. And another. And another.

It is as if they are on a roller coaster and a malicious ride operator has slowed them down in order to prolong their terror.

More time ticks by.

"Hello!" the flyhouse shouts from the other side of the window. "Remember me? Felicity? Part fly? Part house? Dear friend? We've been traveling together? It's getting cold out here! May I come in?"

Seeing as she's not going anywhere, and neither is the car, Mickey opens the window. "Welcome back."

Felicity enters, shivering. "Finally!"

Mickey closes the window and turns back to Shadow. "So why is this not a waterfall?"

"Well, we won't know for sure until we fall—or until we don't fall, I mean," says Shadow, "but I think this is a water-*tall*."

"A what?"

"Technically a water-*rise* or water-*lift*, but you have to admit water-tall sounds better. Water*fall*—water-*tall*, get it?"

"Yeah, it rhymes. But I still don't understand."

Then, waterfall or water-tall, the car finally slips over the edge.

Mickey stifles a scream. He is certain they are about to plunge to their deaths.

But they don't fall; they rise.

Gravity itself seems to have flipped direction. The waterfall has become more like a geyser. It is lifting the car higher and higher.

The windshield now has a view of the sky. They could be in a rocket ship, shooting into space.

"We're flying!" exults Felicity, as if it is her first time.

"Like I said, a water-tall lifts you up," says Shadow to Mickey. "So in a way, it makes you, you know, taller. Makes you older and cooler too. What!!! No, not really. You'll never be cool. What!!! Kidding!"

Mickey wants to respond, but he can barely stop himself from vomiting. It feels like they are in an out-of-control elevator.

But he has to agree: *Water-tall* is as good a word as any to describe it.

Propelled by the water-tall, the car overshoots its landing and for a moment they are sailing in the air.

At last, they land with a loud splash in what appears to be a big pink lake.

Surrounded by ripples, they drift toward shore.

"What happened?" asks Alice quietly. "Are we still alive?"

"I have to get out of this car," says Mickey, holding his stomach with one hand and his mouth with the other.

"No offense," he adds, for Car-Boy's benefit. "It's just that I think I'm going to throw up."

"Can you not throw up long enough to carry me to shore?" asks Alice.

Unsure how to get out of a car that's half-submerged in water, Mickey lowers his window as his sister suggested earlier. He jumps out, holding her above his head.

Happily, his feet touch sand, with the water level just below his shoulders. He's completely soaked, but at least Alice is dry.

The water, it turns out, is not really pink; it's clear. It merely reflects the sky. Which really is pink. Or which appears really to be pink.

"Going for a dip, Mickey?" Felicity buzzes cheerily from above. "I hope you brought a change of clothes."

Ignoring her, Mickey stumbles onto the beach and deposits his sister on the sand. Drenched and dripping, he turns around and vomits into the lake.

Car-Boy guffaws loudly under his hood, making big bubbles in the water; and then rolls onto the beach, water pouring out from all sides.

Only now does Shadow get out. There isn't a drop of water on him. Then again, he still isn't entirely solid. Maybe water just slips right off.

"Welcome to Bad!" he says with a smile.

34.

Bubbles!

"Sorry, man, no cars allowed in Bad," says Shadow, slapping the Camaro on the hood. "A little downtime on the beach? What do you say?"

A sneering growl comes from deep in the car's engine. Camaros, it seems, do not enjoy sunbathing.

"I feel bad for him," Mickey says. "But not too bad."

"You mean, you feel *good* for him," says Shadow. "You're in Bad now. Here bad is good, and good is bad."

"Right."

"Aren't you supposed to say *wrong*?" asks Alice, who is once more perched on Mickey's shoulder. "And what if something isn't good *or* bad? Is blah still blah?"

They start walking up the beach, away from the water.

In the distance looms a mountain that looks as though it has been sprinkled with glittering pink sugar. A stream of giant bubbles rises from the peak like smoke from a volcano.

"That's Bubble Mountain," says Shadow. "Where we're going."

Mickey watches as the wind carries the bubbles toward the shore. All around, bubbles float by, like so many escaped balloons.

"And those bubbles, are they . . ."

"Bubble gum, yup," says Shadow.

The sand too is mostly pink. Mickey picks up a handful and examines it. It looks less like sand than a mass of shiny pebbles.

"And this sand?"

"Also gum. Very old. Fossilized."

As they head inland, more and more bubbles float by.

One sticks to Mickey's shirt until he shakes it off. Another nearly gets caught in his hair.

He hasn't seen this many bubbles since his kindergarten days. Of course, even back then, his mother refused to buy the bottles of bubble solution that everyone else bought. (No single-use plastics!) But she was always happy to make "bubble soup" from soap and water. And she had endless patience with her kids' passion for bubble fights.

He owes his bubble skills to his mother, Mickey thinks now.

This thought leads Mickey to another, less comforting

one: Those very skills are about to be tested in the king's contest.

What if he doesn't win?

Then he probably won't get to meet the king—much less have the chance to ask the king to send them home.

He and his sister will be stuck in the Anti-World forever.

He'll never see his mother again.

Soon, they reach a wide boardwalk devoted, almost entirely, to bubble gum.

The people strolling by show a great deal more variety than the businesses. They are all ages and races and sizes and look as though they've been plucked at random from all corners of the world.

Mickey even spies several animals mingling in the crowd, including a giraffe, a flamingo, and a wild boar.

And yet every face looks vaguely familiar to Mickey, animals not excepted. It is as though everyone has stepped out of his neighborhood mall. Or out of a zoo he once went to.

Mickey leans into Shadow and speaks in an undertone. "Did the Anti-Book create all of these people? It seems impossible. I know I didn't list them all."

"Except you did write *everyone else,* didn't you?" Shadow points out.

Mickey gulps.

There's one thing all the denizens of the boardwalk have in common, human and animal alike: Each and every one is chewing gum, if not blowing a bubble.

"It's kind of weird," says Alice, gripping his collar. "Don't you think? The way they're all chewing. Mickey, are you listening to me?"

He isn't.

Because right in front of them is an enormous mound of bubble gum. Enough to fill a few trucks. Some of the gum comes in sticks, some in cubes, some in balls. There is a rainbow of colors and flavors. There is something, in other words, for everyone. And most especially for Mickey.

Above the mound, on an equally enormous banner, is a portrait of the Bubble Gum King, emblazoned with the words *From your king to you.*

In a daze, Mickey stares at the image of the king while stuffing his mouth to maximum capacity.

Does the king really intend to share his throne with the winner of a chewing gum contest? He looks so imposing, there is no room in his portrait for anyone else. It's hard to imagine him having any heir at all, let alone a kid like Mickey.

As Mickey pops a sixth or seventh gumball into his mouth, Shadow grins at him. "Didn't I tell you Bad was rad? Made for you, am I right?"

Mickey nods, tearing his eyes away from the king.

"But all the people here—they're like professional bubble-blowers!"

His words come out garbled, with a notable lack of hard consonants ("woessiowal uwwle-owers"), but his meaning is clear.

"How can I compete?" he asks, temporarily removing the huge wad of gum from his mouth. "It's a waste of time to even enter the contest."

"That's ridiculous!" Shadow points to a small bubble floating by. "You call this a bubble? Your bubble is gonna kick its little bubble butt."

"Yeah, right," Mickey scoffs, pushing the gum back into his mouth.

Nevertheless, encouraged by Shadow, he flicks the bubble away as if it were no more of a threat than a piece of lint.

Nearly colliding with the bubble, Felicity flies up to Mickey, chattering excitedly.

"Adam is here! Adam is here!"

"Who?"

"Adam! The mime."

"Oh," says Mickey. "You mean Mime-Boy."

"Yes! And he's practically as good as new."

Indeed, a mime that looks very much like Mime-Boy is standing on the boardwalk about twelve yards away, making balloon animals out of bubble-gum bubbles.

"That's not him," says Shadow quickly.

"Yes, it is," says Alice, peering over Mickey's shoulder. "And he's back to normal size. Or skinnier even. I think you shrunk him when you deflated him, Mickey!"

"Told you he'd be fine." Shadow increases his pace. "Come on, let's get you to the castle."

"Wait," says Alice. "I think he's waving at us."

"Check on him later," says Shadow, not stopping. "Let's not be late for the contest. You want to meet the king, right? So you can get big and get home?"

"Yeah, yeah, we do," says Mickey.

Mickey glances back at Mime-Boy. It certainly looks as if he is trying to signal to them.

Felicity hovers in the air, hesitant to leave.

"You folks go ahead," she says. "I'll talk to him. It's the least I can do, after what he's been through."

"Okay, thanks!" says Mickey, relieved to not have to choose between checking on the mime and keeping up with their guide.

35.

Bad news!

"Extra! Extra! Read all about it! New proclamations from the king!"

As they inch closer to the base of Bubble Mountain, a crowd forms on the sidewalk, blocking their path.

"What's going on?" asks Mickey.

"Bad News," says Shadow.

Alice frowns. "Oh no, what happened?"

Shadow laughs. "No, that's the name of the newspaper. *The Bad News.* The paperboy is here with the new edition."

"Newspaper? I want to see," says Alice.

With his sister prodding him, Mickey pushes his way into the crowd. In the middle is a boy made of paper, standing next to a tall stack of newspapers.

"Get your new news before it becomes old news!" the paperboy cries, handing out papers to eager customers.

"Remember: What's bad news today may be good news tomorrow!"

Mickey takes a copy of *The Bad News* and holds it up so his sister can read it.

On the front page, in the left-hand column, there is an article by the king. In the right-hand column, there is another article by the king. But it's upside down.

Mickey turns the paper over. It is the same article as the first.

Alice shades her eyes with her hand and reads to Mickey as he walks.

It Is So Because I Say So!
by the Bubble Gum King

To all my subjects, good, bad, or otherwise:

Henceforward and forever after, until I change my mind, I proclaim the following to be false, that is to say, true.

Bad is the new bad. But it is still the old bad. Therefore, since the old bad was good, good is still bad. In other words, all is bad in Bad.

Left is the new right. Right is the new wrong. Blue is the new red. Red is the new yellow. Yellow is the new hello. Hello is the new goodbye.

New is the new old. Old is the new new. Entertainment is the new science. Science is the new fantasy. Fantasy is the new reality. Chew is the new swallow. Hungry is the new full.

Fear is the new hope. Hate is the new love.

And lastly, never forget, what's mine is yours,
but what's yours is mine. So all is mine.

Mine. Mine. Mine.

"Is this guy for real? Must be kinda hard to keep up around here," Alice comments when she's done reading. "I hope he can stop switching left and right long enough to tell us how to get normal and go home."

By now they've reached the tall pink wall that surrounds the base of the Bubble Gum Mountain.

Big posters hang on the wall, with the King's proclamations emblazoned on them:

In the center is a big iron gate that looks impenetrable.

"Um, are you sure the contest is inside?" asks Mickey, getting more and more nervous.

"Just chill for a sec," says Shadow. "First, I gotta go see a guy about a thing."

Mickey eyes him suspiciously. "What thing?"

"The contest, dummy. I gotta sign you up."

As Shadow walks away, two big, mangy, menacing dogs approach. They wear knit ski masks pulled down over their faces, as if they are about to rob a bank. One dog carries a bucket in his mouth, the other a long stick.

"This can't be good," Mickey whispers to his sister.

But the dogs pass them without so much as a glance in their direction.

As Mickey and Alice watch in fascination, the dogs stop beneath one of the posters. The dog with the stick sniffs the air—checking for danger—then dips his stick into the other dog's bucket. When he removes it, the end is covered in gold paint. The stick is a paintbrush.

Still holding the paintbrush in his mouth, the dog jumps onto the back of his companion, stands up on his hind legs, and quickly proceeds to paint over the poster's message.

THE DOODLER SAYS
LOVE IS ~~HATE~~ LOVE

Finished, the dogs check their surroundings one last time, then disappear as quickly as they arrived.

"Smart dogs," observes Alice. "Can you imagine Noodle doing graffiti?"

"Sure," says Mickey. "What about his Noodle doodles?"

"You mean his paw prints," says Alice. "Well, who knows what the anti-version of him is like. He could be super smart."

"*Or* he could've turned into an actual noodle."

Alice giggles. "A pasta pet! Just like you thought when you were little . . . You and that dog loved each other so much. I was so jealous."

"Of me or the dog?"

"Both!"

"Really?" Mickey asks.

He never imagined his sister caring enough to be jealous.

"Hey, Mickey," Alice says after a moment. "Why does it feel like we got a divorce at the same time our parents did?"

"Oh, I dunno. Maybe because you abandoned me for your boyfriend and your oh-so-mature teenage life."

"I did not!" says Alice.

Then, "Okay, maybe I did. A little."

"Well, thanks for admitting it, at least."

"I think it's because you remind me of how sad I am about Mom and Dad, and I don't want to think about it."

Mickey nods. He doesn't like to think about it either.

"Why'd you have to pick somebody like Car-Boy, though?" he asks. "Sean, I mean. You're so smart. And he's so . . . I just don't get it."

"Sometimes I don't get it either." Alice shakes her head ruefully. "Maybe that's the point. He's just so different from our family. Part of my get-away-as-far-as-I-can plan."

"Not that far away," Mickey notes. "Just down the block."

"True." Alice smiles mischievously. "Admit it, though. He *is* pretty good-looking. Well, before he turned into a car."

"I guess," says Mickey reluctantly.

Whether or not he thinks Car-Boy is good-looking is a subject he'd much rather avoid.

Alice pokes Mickey. "You're still my best little brother."

"*You're* the little one now."

"No! Say it right."

"Okay," Mickey says with an exaggerated sigh. "I'm your *only* little brother."

Alice nods. That's more like it. "And then . . . ?"

"You're my best big sister," Mickey says dutifully.

"I'm your *only* big sister," Alice replies on cue.

Mickey smiles down at her. "Happy now?"

"Yes," says Alice. "I would give you a big big-sister hug but it's kind of hard with these little arms. So here's a little big-sister hug." She puts her arms around his neck—or around a very small portion of his neck.

"Little big-sister hug accepted," says Mickey. "But could you let go now? That kind of tickles."

"Oh, look—the Copy Cats!" says his sister, letting go of him. "Are they the same ones from before?"

Mickey shrugs. "No clue. But they don't look very happy."

Two uniformed tabbies have arrived at the site of the graffiti. They open up a supply sack and take out their own paintbrush and bucket. In a moment, the sign's original message is restored:

LOVE IS ~~HATE~~ ~~LOVE~~ HATE

"Bend down," says Alice. "I want to get off."

Straddling his arm, she slides to the ground.

"At least I can ask if they've seen our dog anywhere," she says, dusting herself off.

"I dunno," says Mickey. "Something tells me you don't want to ask a cat about a dog."

But she is already running down the block, his warning unheard or unheeded.

The Copy Cats arch their backs in surprise when the three-inch-tall girl approaches.

As Alice talks, they circle her as if she is a trapped mouse. Mickey can't hear what Alice is saying, but the cats' purrs are just loud enough to decipher.

"Noodle? What kind of name is Noodle? And where did you last see this so-called Noodle?"

"Tell me, how does a nice girl like you get involved with riffraff like that?"

"Oh, a nice dog, you say? Sorry, no such thing. Brutes! Every one of them . . ."

Concerned, Mickey starts walking in the cats' direction.

"Why not file a missing dog report at the station? Unless there's something you're trying to hide?"

"Just come with us. We'll give you a lift . . ."

The cat facing Alice nods to the cat behind her. As Mickey watches in horror, the second cat lunges for Alice, bites into the back of her neck, and lifts her off the ground as if she were a baby kitten—or dinner.

"Wait! That's my sister!" Mickey yells, sprinting after them.

Alice swings wildly from the cat's mouth, shrieking. "Let me down! You can't do this! What's your badge number? Help! Mickey!"

Mickey runs as fast as he can, but not fast enough. Just as he's about to catch up, the cats disappear in a crack between two buildings.

Frantic, he runs around the block, but he sees no sign of his sister or the Copy Cats. Just a few bubbles bobbing in the breeze.

When Shadow returns, Mickey is slumped against the pink wall, panting and miserable.

Mickey breathlessly relays what happened.

"They must have thought she was working for the Doodler," says Shadow.

"But she's not even from this world," says Mickey. "That's crazy!"

Shadow shakes his head. "Not so crazy. The Doodler has spies everywhere. But don't worry, she'll be fine. Unless they're hungry. What!!! Kidding! They won't eat her. Probably. As soon as they figure out who she is, they'll take her straight to the king."

"Well, can we go straight to the king too? Oh, no—wait," says Mickey faltering. "What about the contest?"

Shadow smiles. "That's the good news."

"What is?"

"You lost!"

"That's good news?"

"Well, *lost* in the sense of *won*. I should have said that's the *bad* news."

Now Mickey is even more confused. "How could I win? It hasn't even happened yet."

"I know, right?" Shadow can barely contain his excitement. "I went to sign you up. Turns out that you, my dude, were the only contestant. So you automatically have the high score. Lowest score too, if that's better . . . How cool is that?"

"Why didn't they just cancel it?"

"Would you want to be the person to tell the king that nobody entered his contest?"

"Uh . . ."

"I didn't think so! Anyways, what did I tell you about looking a gift contest in the mouth? Take the win. Be the guy. Heir to the Anti-Throne. Awesome ruler in training. Etcetera. Etcetera."

Shadow bows theatrically. "I bow to you, Your Almost Highness."

Mickey cracks a smile. "Thanks, Your, um, Lowness."

Shadow laughs appreciatively. "Wait, was that a burn? You're learning, my friend."

"It was a burn," says Mickey, enjoying the praise more than he probably should under the circumstances. "So can we go see the king now? I don't want to have to tell my parents that a cat ate my sister."

"Just your homework, right?" jokes Shadow.

Mickey tries to smile again, but he can't. It wasn't so long ago that fighting with his mom over homework was the worst part of his day.

36.

His Royal Bubbliciousness.

Mickey always thought that flying in a hot-air balloon would be a relaxing experience, like floating in a pool. But the contraption he is currently riding in is nothing like the gentle airship he imagined.

Of course, in this case, the balloon is not a balloon but an oversized bubble-gum bubble.

As he and Shadow make their way to the top of Bubble Mountain, they bounce and swing with alarming force. Mickey looks down at the sharp rocks that cover the mountainside below, then at the column of heat keeping the bubble afloat.

"Are you sure the bubble won't melt?" he asks Shadow.

"No."

"Oh." Mickey swallows.

"The trick is to land before that happens."

Smiling, Shadow nods to their destination: Just below the mountaintop stands the residence of the Bubble Gum King.

From a distance, it could be a well-preserved castle from the Middle Ages—in France, or Scotland, maybe. But the closer they get, the more unreal it looks.

It is less a castle than a four-year-old's fantasy of a castle—with turrets and domes covered in silver stars and purple stripes. Like you might find on the cover of a picture book, with a dragon flying above it. Or come to think of it, on a T-shirt Mickey had when he was little, with a unicorn grazing in the background.

Mickey is not sure whether to be attracted or repelled.

Castle guards—uniformed cats holding bayonets— walk the parapets. They all turn in unison when Shadow and Mickey disembark.

Mickey swallows. Their inscrutable expressions are extremely intimidating.

Shadow steps ahead of Mickey and whispers to two of the guards. The cats' eyes go wide, and they immediately beckon Mickey forward.

"When you see the king, show some respect, okay?" says Shadow as one of the cats escorts them through the castle doors.

"He's the king, why wouldn't I?" answers Mickey.

"Just slip in a little compliment or two. Your Awesome Bubbliness to the Max, or whatever."

"Um, okay," says Mickey, not at all certain that he will be able to flatter the king properly. "Oh, darn—I never got a gift for him!"

"Don't worry," says Shadow. "If he wants something from you, he'll tell you."

The interior of the castle is a surprise. The surprise is that so much of it has yet to exist.

At first, Mickey mistakes the holes in the walls for windows. But as he walks deeper into the castle, he sees that the holes are, instead, un-built parts of the building.

Looking around corners and peeking through doorways, he discovers rooms that are missing walls, and walls that are missing rooms. It looks as if the builder got bored and wandered away, like a kid abandoning a video game before she's finished constructing her new digital mansion.

Mickey wants to ask for an explanation, but Shadow won't stop talking about the king.

"Oh, and never stand too close to him!" warns Shadow. "That's super important."

"I don't get it," says Mickey. "Aren't you going in to see the king with me?"

"Me? Never." Shadow laughs with uncharacteristic nervousness.

Mickey looks at him sideways. "I thought you said you guys were buddies."

"We are! In a way. He's the king. He's everyone's buddy, right?"

Mickey is incredulous. "So you don't really know him? What else did you lie about? What about all those nicknames?" he asks, growing slightly hysterical. "What about me winning the contest? Did you make that up too?"

"Chill, dude," whispers Shadow. "Trust me, he'll want to see you. You're the anti-hero, remember?"

"What does that have to do with it?"

"Well, you have the Anti-Book, for one."

Before Mickey can press Shadow any further, their escort stops in front of an open door guarded by two more cats. "The throne room, sir."

The doorway is tall and terrifying, and Mickey really, really doesn't want to meet the king alone, but his unreliable friend has already slipped away.

Mickey tells himself to be brave for his sister.

At first, Mickey thinks he's entered the wrong room, or at least come at the wrong time. Because the king sits not on a throne but on a barber's chair. Likewise, his shoulders are draped not with a red velvet cape but with a black cloth.

The guards nudge Mickey forward.

As Mickey approaches, the king is looking at himself in a hand mirror. Standing on his shoulders are two squirrels in barbers' aprons. One on each side, they carefully twirl the ends of his long mustache.

A third squirrel stands on a side table, vigorously polishing a gold crown.

"Excuse me, Your Bubbleness, is our work to your satisfaction?" asks the squirrel on the king's left.

Sucking in his cheeks, the king turns to one side, then the other, inspecting himself from all angles. The squirrels watch his every movement, their whiskers twitching with anxiety.

"Twirlers," he says finally, "this mustache is a masterpiece. I dare say, *I* am a masterpiece."

The squirrels breathe audible sighs of relief. "Thank you, Your Bubbliness! You *are* a masterpiece! Yes!"

Mickey is inclined to agree: The king's mustache looks like a work of art. So does the king himself. That is to say, he looks exactly like his picture. He could almost be a wax model made to resemble the image on a bubble-gum package.

From this distance, at least, he appears not to be flesh and blood. The entire scene is quite eerie.

Meanwhile, the king continues to gaze at the mirror. "Hmm. *Mustache is the new beard?* Or maybe *Mustaches are the new lips?* No, I've got it . . ." He points to his reflection. "*You are the new me.* That's it! Did you get that, Secret-tary?"

A gray cat in sunglasses and a trench coat looks up from his notes and purrs his assent. "Yes, Your Bubbleness."

"Write it everywhere," says the king, not taking his eyes off of the mirror. "*Everyone* will be the new me!"

Mickey coughs nervously. "Excuse me, Your Bubbleness?" he says, imitating the squirrels.

The king makes a funny face, then a serious one,

obviously very fascinated by his reflection. "Or should it be *I am the new you*?"

Mickey tries again. "Your Double Bubble-ness? Your Bubbliciousness?"

"Hmmmm . . ." says the king. It is unclear whether he is addressing Mickey or himself.

The bubble-gum contest may have been canceled, but Mickey is being put through a test of a different kind.

"Your Super Deluxe With a Cherry On Top Royal Bubble Double-ness?"

"Hmph?" The king is still not looking at Mickey, but at least he seems to be acknowledging Mickey's existence.

"Your Super Duper Extra Deluxe With Chocolate Sprinkles, Cookie Crumbs, Gummy Bears, and Twelve Cherries, Bubble Gumminess?"

"Yes? Get on with it!" snaps the king. "You're making me ill."

"Oh, sorry! I'm Mickey, the, um, contest winner, er, loser? I mean loser! Not that the contest ever . . . Well, I'm from the real world, and—"

"THE WHERE?!" The king's words are so loud, he seems to rise from his seat.

"The fake world! The fake world!" Mickey corrects himself in a panic.

"Ah, you must mean the *pre–Anti-World*," says the king, settling down.

"Right! That!" Mickey agrees desperately. "Anyway, I really love . . . gum. It's . . . you're my favorite brand."

"*I* am?"

"Well, your brand is my favorite."

The king smiles for the first time. "Then you have very fine taste. What's your favorite flavor?"

"Um . . ." Mickey hesitates. What's the right answer?

"How can you choose, right?" says the king, nodding in understanding. "But really, tell me, which is it? I so seldom get to talk to my customers. You're my focus group of one. Blueberry Blast-off? Strawberry Super Burst? Cinnamon Firebomb?"

"Um, bubble-gum flavor?" Mickey squeaks.

The king's eyes narrow. "What's wrong with the others?"

"Nothing! They're great! Every one of them. They're really super . . . flavorful. It's just that I like bubble gum best. Because bubbles, I guess? Sorry. My fault. I'm boring."

"Relax. I'm just giving you a hard time." The king chuckles. "You're a traditionalist. I like that. So many young people today don't appreciate the classics."

Mickey nods vehemently. "I know. Young people. So unappreciative."

The king glances at the squirrels, and they scurry to the side of the room, giving the king and Mickey more space.

"Come here, son," says the king. "So I can see you better."

Mickey nervously steps toward the king. Before he

can take a second step, the king raises a hand. "Not too close! Ha-ha. The mustache, you know! Not to be touched."

The squirrels advance on Mickey, baring their teeth in a threatening manner. The king waves them away.

"So Your . . . Bubbliness," says Mickey tentatively. "I wanted to ask about my sister."

The king strokes his mustache. "Let me guess. Three inches tall. Red hair. Yellow headphones?"

"Yes! So you've seen her!" Mickey is flooded with relief.

"Never in my life."

"Oh," says Mickey, confused. "Well, has anyone else—"

"That was a joke," says the king. "Don't they have jokes where you're from? She's here. In the castle."

"She is? That's . . . that's great!" says Mickey, looking around. "She's not a prisoner, is she? Because that was a mistake! She doesn't work for the Doodler. She's never even met him," he explains in a rush. "All she wants is to go back to her regular size and go back to the real world. Me too. I'm ready to—"

The king's eyes flare. "The *real* world again, is it?"

"I mean, the pre—"

"*THIS* IS THE REAL WORLD!"

"Right. Right. Sorry." Mickey cowers, sure he's about to be thrown out of the throne room—or worse.

"Forgive me, I'm a little stressed." The king takes a breath, forcing himself to calm down. "What I'm trying to say is, what's the rush to go back? What did that old pathetic pre–Anti-World of yours ever do for you? You had such wonderful friends?"

"Well, no . . . n-not really," Mickey stammers.

"Such a close, loving family?"

"Um, sorta? It's complicated."

"Exactly. Who needs the headache?"

"Well, they're not *just* a headache," says Mickey.

"Weren't you planning on divorcing your parents?"

"Yeah, but . . ." Mickey stumbles. How does everyone in the Anti-World know so much about him?

"But what? Stay here! We could use a guy like you in the Anti-World. *I* could use a guy like you."

"What could you ever need *me* for?" Mickey scoffs.

"Don't sell yourself short, Mickey," says the king warmly. "You've got all kinds of things to offer."

"Like what?"

"Kings are people, too. We need friends and family, like everyone does. Why do you think I held that contest? Which I am so glad you won, er, lost." The king's eyes moisten with feeling. "It is the great tragedy of my life that I have no child of my own. Stay in the Anti-World, Mickey. You will be my son and heir."

He opens his arms as if about to give Mickey a fatherly hug, then lowers them when Mickey stays put.

"Think about it," says the king. "You will no longer be Mickey, the kid from a broken home, abandoned by his parents. The kid they call names and throw things at. You will be the Bubble Gum Prince. Powerful and adored."

So far the Bubble Gum King has seemed by turns terrifying and ridiculous. But suddenly Mickey feels . . . what? Sympathy and something else. Sure, the king is vain and eccentric, but he also seems genuinely to want Mickey to be his son.

Unlike Mickey's real father.

His father is starting a new family. Why can't Mickey?

The king is right. What's waiting for Mickey at home, really? Except a lot of anxiety and recrimination. For all Mickey knows, he'll be thrown in jail for what he did with the Anti-Book. Or sent right back to the Anti-World!

"And of course you'll have all the gum you want," promises the king.

Mickey tries to picture life as the king's son. The castle is big and grand, yes. But very empty.

"I like gum, I mean, I really like it," says Mickey awkwardly. "But people need other things too—you know, to live."

"Other than gum?! What else is there?"

Mickey shrinks back, regretting his words. "Um, like food or whatever, I guess?"

The king smiles. "Kidding! Gum isn't everything. Even I know that. Whatever you want, it's yours. Your own castle? A car that has four legs instead of two arms? Or would you prefer wheels?"

"Wheels, I think." Mickey laughs.

"What about my sister?" he asks, coming back to reality. "She won't want to stay. You have to let her out now."

The king frowns at him. "I wasn't aware that I *had* to do anything."

"Sorry!" exclaims Mickey, his face pale. Why does he keep saying the wrong thing? "It's just that I promised you could help her."

"Yes, yes, soon, soon," says the king. "First, you must help me."

"How?"

"Bring me the Doodler."

"The Doodler?"

The king nods gravely. "Our differences are tearing my kingdom apart. We must make peace at any cost."

"How am I supposed to bring him to you? I don't even know him."

"My informants tell me otherwise. They say you are the one person who can convince him to go with you."

Mickey wrinkles his face in confusion. Why would anyone say that?

"Tell the Doodler that you are on a mission of peace and that he is invited here as a friend," says the king. "In the meantime, you can leave the Anti-Book with me. As a little security deposit. Guard!"

The king snaps his fingers and one of the cats trots over. Hissing at Mickey, the cat holds out a paw.

For a second, Mickey considers writing *CAT* in the Anti-Book. But making the king's guard disappear would likely not be the best way to stay in the king's good graces.

Reluctantly, he takes the Anti-Book out of his pocket and hands it over.

"Can I take my sister with me at least?" he asks.

"Much too dangerous," says the king. "We'll keep her safe here. Besides, I don't have any pets, only these animals," he adds, indicating the squirrels.

"My sister is not a pet!" Mickey protests.

But it's too late. He is already being escorted out.

part four and a half:

worse

37.

The worst!

Mickey finds Shadow leaning against a castle wall, enjoying the sun. He remains frustratingly calm, even when Mickey tells him about the king's orders.

"No worries, man," says Shadow. "We'll just bring him the Doodler, like he said. Then—boom!—you're the prince. Your sister goes home. And everyone lives happily ever after."

"But I don't even know where to look!" Mickey insists. To him the situation could not be more dire.

"That's easy," says Shadow. "We just have to go from Bad to Worse."

"Worse?"

"Uh-huh. Everyone knows that's where the Doodler hides out. Now, I don't want to freak you out or anything, but Worse is the worst."

"Meaning it's the best?" Mickey asks hopefully.

"Sorry, dude. It's worst as in *worst*. But it's a quick trip. We'll be back in a flash."

As it turns out, the trip down the mountain is even more harrowing than the trip up.

Instead of a hot-air bubble-balloon, they ride in what looks like a ski gondola made from the bottom half of a giant gumdrop shell.

Mickey stares up at the thin cord that supports the gondola's weight. With every movement of the gondola, the cord expands and contracts like a rubber band.

"That string—it's stretched-out gum, isn't it?"

"Yup," says Shadow.

Mickey nods, biting his lip. He's always found Bubble Gum King bubble gum to be pretty tough, but he's never before hung from a string of it.

When they near the bottom, they enter a dark tunnel, only to emerge seconds later in harsh bright light.

Mickey turns to look back at Bubble Mountain and for the first time he sees that the mountain, as well as the lake on the other side of it, is encased in a gigantic pink bubble.

"So that's why the sky looked pink! It's like a snow globe for giants."

"Pretty much," agrees Shadow. "And we're on the outside now."

On the outside is right. As far as Mickey can tell, Worse is nothing more than a garbage dump for Bad. The streets are littered with so many wads of gum that his shoes stick to the ground with every step.

"Did you know that in Singapore chewing gum is illegal?" he says, to fill the silence. "It's because they don't want any gum dropped on the street."

"Yeah?" Shadow doesn't seem to be listening.

Vendors line the sidewalk, selling misshapen lumps that may have once been fruits or vegetables, but no longer look the least bit edible.

"Get your bad apples here!" shouts one vendor.

"Bad eggs for sale!" shouts another, holding up a blackened ball. "Come have a sniff, friend. It only looks like it's gone good!"

"Don't go near them," Shadow warns Mickey. "It will make you sick. I mean, well."

"Don't worry, I'm not tempted."

As they get deeper into Worse, Mickey notices more and more graffiti covering the walls, most of it in gold.

THE DOODLER IS OUR DUDE
STAND BY YOUR PACK
KINGS RULE BUT WE DROOL!
BE A LOVER NOT A BITER

Despite these warm sentiments, Mickey feels more and more uneasy. He knows they're being watched.

And, more to the point, smelled.

More than one dog has sniffed in their direction, then barked loudly into the distance, seemingly signaling comrades about the presence of strangers in the street.

One building appears to have escaped the graffiti artists. It is an all-red wooden structure with a peaked roof and a large arched entry. Two dogs lie in front, scratching themselves like strays, but Mickey detects a certain wariness in their expressions.

"That's where you're going," whispers Shadow.

"It looks like a doghouse," Mickey whispers back. "But the size of a human house."

"It *is* a doghouse. You go ahead. Best for me to keep a low profile around here."

"Why's that?" Mickey asks. But Shadow has already retreated into the background.

As Mickey nears the doghouse, the dogs stand up and block the entry.

"Hey, bub. You lost?" asks a scruffy dog in a knit beanie.

"Or you just looking for trouble?" asks his buddy.

Mickey thinks it might be one of the dogs who wrote over the king's LOVE IS HATE sign, but he isn't sure.

"I don't think so," says Mickey, feeling increasingly anxious. "I'm looking for the Doodler."

"Is that right?" says the dog, sniffing suspiciously. "And what makes you think the Doodler is here? From what I've heard, he doesn't exist. He's just a bedtime story."

"But I really, really need to speak to him," says Mickey.

"If he *does* exist, do you have any idea where I might find him?"

"I might, I might not . . ."

The dog looks at his colleague, who growls disinterestedly. They don't seem very inclined to help.

Then comes a booming voice:

"Who goes there? I know that smell!"

38.

You're the Doodler?!

Mickey sees a flash of gold.

Next thing he knows he's on the ground, and a slobbering dog is licking his face with a big wet tongue.

"I knew you'd come!" exults the dog. "I knew it! I knew it!"

"Noodle? Is that you?" asks Mickey when he's able to sit up and take a breath. "*You're* the Doodler?!"

"I know, right?" says the dog, between happy barks. "Can you believe it? Hometown dog makes good, and all that jazz. Come on in!"

As Mickey follows Noodle's wagging tail inside, he sees that his dog is much the same as he remembers. Noodle hasn't turned into a noodle. But his coat has a new sparkle, his paws a new glint, his eyes a new gleam.

He looks like the same old Noodle—dipped in twenty-four-karat gold.

"So what do you think, man?" asks the golden golden doodle, taking a seat on an oversized purple satin doggy bed. He waves a gold paw, as if showing off jewelry. "Too flashy?"

"No, I like it," says Mickey cautiously.

"Not a bad gig for an old dog, huh?" Noodle nods to the piles of dog treats, bones, and torn socks that surround him like offerings at a shrine.

Around the edges of the room, a motley assortment of dogs sit at attention. They appear to be awaiting Noodle's instructions.

"Did you get the gifts I left for you?" the dog asks eagerly. "Did you? Did you?"

"What gifts?" asks Mickey.

"The golden gifts!" says Noodle. "I left a trail for you. You must have found them. Why else would you be here?"

"Oh, the gold poops! Right. Yeah. I have a . . . friend who really likes them."

Where is Felicity, anyway? Mickey wonders. He misses her hovering presence.

"A *friend*? Sure, sure. Let go of the shame, man."

Laughing, Noodle turns to his dog minions, and points back at Mickey with his paw.

"This guy, he's a total nut," says Noodle affectionately. "He loves my turds. Can't get enough of them. He wraps them in these special bags, and drops them in these special treasure bins he keeps around the neighborhood. You'd think I pooped gold. Hey, that's a good one!"

Mickey looks at him in confusion. "Treasure bins? You mean trash cans?"

"Trash cans?" The dog looks back at Mickey, equally confused. "Like for getting rid of stuff?"

"That's what trash is," agrees Mickey.

"What are you saying? So all that time, you weren't keeping my turds?"

Mickey shakes his head. "Sorry."

"Well, that's just . . ." Noodle barks unhappily. "Those turds were my gifts to you. Maybe they weren't always gold, but they were mine! And you tossed them away like garbage?"

The other dogs howl with outrage.

"I can see how that might seem kind of rude," says Mickey, looking around nervously. "But that's what humans do."

Noodle shakes his head in disgust. "Next thing you're going to tell me that when you throw me a ball, I'm not supposed to keep it!"

"Actually, you're supposed to bring it back—it's called *fetch*. But forget that!" Mickey says quickly. "Next time, keep the ball."

The dog stares at him. "What kind of guy gives you a present as nice as a ball and then expects you to give it back?! That's just cruel."

Noodle's canine minions nod their heads in angry agreement.

Mickey bites his lip. This meeting is not going well. "Sorry, man, I don't know what to say."

"Who you calling 'man'? I'm not even man's best friend, judging by you! Bye. I gotta meditate." Noodle nods to the other dogs. "Brothers and sisters, it's time to practice our mindfulness."

The dogs whine balefully, but Noodle quiets them with a sharp bark. "I know meditation is hard, but in the end it makes life so much easier."

In seconds, all the dogs are sitting upright with their paws in front of them and their eyes closed.

Panic-stricken, Mickey doesn't move. If he can't convince Noodle to leave with him, he may as well not return to the king. And he can forget about ever seeing his sister again.

"I'm really, really sorry," he says desperately. "You're right. It's terrible the way people treat dogs. I should have known those turds were gifts."

Noodle opens his eyes and grins. "No worries. I'm over it already. Let's shake."

The dog holds out a paw, then snatches it back when Mickey reaches for it. Mickey's hand is left hanging in the air.

Noodle laugh-barks like a hyena. "Hehehe. You humans and your handshakes."

"You got me," says Mickey.

The other dogs are laughing at him too. "Shake" jokes are clearly popular with this crowd.

"So all these other dogs, they're like your followers?" Mickey asks.

"Totally bonkers, right? *I'm* the alpha. Me! Noodle!" Noodle shakes his head in amazement. "They think I'm a god! A real doggone god. And guess what, maybe I am. And not just because I'm all gold and shiny. The way I look at it, every dog is a god. I mean, what is *D-O-G* but *G-O-D* backward? Coincidence? Come on."

Not a coincidence in this case anyway, thinks Mickey. Because *D-O-G* is what I wrote in the Anti-Book, and a *G-O-D* is what you became.

"Here's the thing, though," continues Noodle. "I may not be the biggest dog in the kennel, or the smartest, or even the cutest or cuddliest (although, don't get me wrong, I like me a good cuddle!), but, god or not, you know what I've got?"

"What?"

"A heart!" Noodle nods to the other dogs in the room. "Just like she's got. And she's got. And he's got. And we've all got. It's all about the love, my friend. *L-O-V-E*. Love."

At this, all the dogs in the room woof and cheer. "Right on!"

"That's what I'm talking about!"

"Love is love!"

"See what I mean?" says Noodle. "They lap it up. They're hungry for it."

"Wow, well, congratulations," says Mickey. "That's really . . . cool."

The love talk is making Mickey uncomfortable. It reminds him of his sister, who is a prisoner—because of him. His parents, who may no longer exist—because of him. And even Noodle himself, the dog whose gifts he rejected.

He wants to make amends, but can he?

"So this might sound weird," says Mickey, "but I'm actually here for a reason."

"You don't need a reason," says Noodle. "I'm your dog; you're my human. What did I just tell you about love?"

"I know, but I have a reason anyway," says Mickey. "I want to take you somewhere."

"You want to take me on a walk?" Trembling with excitement, Noodle immediately heads for the door. "Far out! I love walks!"

Mickey follows, smiling weakly. "Well, technically, yeah. A walk. To the castle."

Noodle stops in the doorway. "The *castle* castle? Like, the king's castle?"

"That's the one."

"Nope. No, sir. No way."

"But we have to," says Mickey urgently. "I promised the king—"

"Maybe you don't understand," says Noodle, backing into the room. "Me and the king, we don't see things the same. I'm a lover. He's a hater. We're at war, you could say."

"But that's just it. He wants to make peace."

"Peace?" Noodle hesitates.

"Yes, peace! He wants to unite the kingdom. He says you're invited to the castle as a friend."

"A friend, huh?" Noodle shakes his head, struggling with himself. "I never like to turn down a paw offered in friendship."

"Well, that's what he's offering! The paw of friendship."

"Besides," says Noodle, turning around, "I'd go anywhere with you, Mickey, you know that."

"Great," says Mickey, exhaling. "Thanks."

As they exit the Doodler's compound together, Shadow greets them. "Yo, Doodler, what's up? I'm Shadow."

Mickey braces himself. Is Noodle going to say hello, or is he going to jump on Shadow and lick his face?

He does neither. He growls. A low, threatening growl. A growl Mickey has never heard before.

"Hey, easy, Noodle," says Mickey. "This is my buddy. He's taking us to the castle."

"Your buddy? This guy?" Noodle lowers his voice. Mickey bends down to hear him. "I don't like to say it, Mickey, but he's no good. He . . . he has no smell!"

"Oh, come on, that's not his fault," says Mickey, standing. "Shadow's not a bad guy. He wants to be friends too."

"He does, huh?" The dog walks back and forth between Mickey and Shadow, sniffing cautiously.

"Sure I do," says Shadow.

"Okay then—friends," says Noodle. "Shake on it?"

He offers his paw, then drops it when Shadow extends his hand.

"Ha! A joker!" says Shadow good-naturedly.

Noodle laughs. "Gets 'em every time!"

No longer worried, he wags his tail as the three of them walk toward Bubble Mountain.

Everything I said was true, Mickey thinks, looking guiltily at his dog. So why do I feel so dishonest?

39.

His Royal Bubbliciousness— part two.

"Are you sure you won't go in?" Mickey asks Shadow when they reach the door to the throne room. "I know the king's a little nuts, but I'm sure if I asked—"

"Forget it. Knock yourself out. You and the pooch," says Shadow, sauntering away. "I'll hang out outside."

Noodle looks anxiously from Shadow to Mickey. "Where is he going? I knew this was a bad idea. Let's go back to my house."

"We can't," says Mickey. "What about the peace mission? The king's expecting us!"

"I am, indeed!" shouts the king from inside. "Come on in!"

Mickey gives Noodle a *What did I tell you?* look, and leads the dog into the throne room.

"Welcome back, Mickey, my son! And who's that handsome dog with you? Don't tell me *he's* the Doodler? That golden fur is fit for a king. I must confess I'm a little jealous."

Black barber cloth gone, the king now wears a velvet cape trimmed in fur. He strokes it as if considering what the cape would look like in gold.

The barber chair too is gone, replaced by an enormous upholstered throne, so plush and wide, it could be a couch. The king pats the cushion on either side.

"Come here, both of you. Sit!"

Seeing Mickey take a seat, Noodle jumps onto the throne. Trying not to get too close to the king, he looks around skeptically, sniffing the air for hidden dangers.

"See, Mickey—I knew you could bring him to me! Have faith in yourself." Smiling broadly, the king claps Mickey on the back. "Isn't this something? Just like a family sitting down to watch TV or play charades."

Sort of like that, Mickey thinks. Sort of not. And why does everybody keep bringing up charades?

"Your family is your pack," observes Noodle. "Pack means love."

"Oh, there you go with your 'love' stuff," says the king. "Can we agree there will be no more of that?"

"No more love?" asks the dog, distressed. "But I thought you wanted peace. Love means peace."

"Sure, sure. But no more *Doodler says this* or *Doodler says that*. It confuses my subjects and it makes me happy. And when I say *happy* I don't mean *happy*. Am I clear?"

The distinctly unhappy Noodle shakes his head. "Happy isn't happy?"

"Never mind. Soon you won't have to worry your silly doggy head about it."

Very stiffly, the king pats the dog's back. "Who's a good dog?" he says in a rough approximation of the way people normally talk to dogs.

"Good is good?" asks Noodle, who is looking more and more worried.

Mickey glances apologetically at Noodle. "Sure, good is good . . . Right, Your, er, Bubbliciousness? Speaking of family, can I see my sister now?"

"All in good time, son. Or all in bad time." The king turns to the dog. "No, in answer to your question, good is not good."

His face suddenly serious, the king snaps his fingers. "Squirrels! Take this dog away."

In seconds, two squirrels drop onto Noodle from the top of the throne. They slip a muzzle over his mouth and a choke collar onto his neck.

"What are you doing? Stop!" cries Mickey, outraged. "You can't do that! You said this was a peace mission!"

He lunges at the squirrels, but another squirrel comes up behind him and points a sword at his neck.

"Oh no you don't," the squirrel snarls in his ear.

"Don't be naive," says the king. "You know I can't have a nasty little dog like that running around my anti-kingdom, spreading his so-called 'truth,' planting his lovey-dovey ideas in people's heads."

Tugging on a leash, a team of twelve squirrels pulls the whimpering and confused dog out of the room.

Mickey watches helplessly. "Please. Let me have him back. I'll take him and my sister and we'll return to our world and you won't have to see any of us ever again."

"Nonsense," says the king. "You're not going anywhere. We had an agreement."

"The agreement was if I brought you the Doodler, you'd help us do whatever we wanted," says Mickey, panic slowly overtaking him.

"I'm sorry, you misunderstood," says the king, not the least bit regretfully. "There's no way out of the Anti-World. You can't undo the Anti-Book any more than you can put a bubble back together once it pops."

"Um . . ." Mickey is about to say he saw somebody do precisely that earlier, but he thinks better of it.

"You already tried to un-write the book," the king reminds him. "You erased your list of words. And where did that get you? It got you here."

"How do you know about that?"

The king raises an eyebrow, as if to say, *I know everything.*

Mickey looks around, desperate. Somewhere in the castle Alice is being held prisoner.

"If you want, I'll stay," he says to the king. "I'll do anything. Please—just send my sister back. And my dog."

"Hmm . . ." The king twists his mustache thoughtfully. "There *is* one thing you could do. It might be a bit scary, but it would make all the difference."

"Yeah?"

"If you do this last little task for me, I'll give you what you ask. Your sister, your dog, everything."

"So you *can* send us back! What is it?"

"Write your name in the Anti-Book."

Mickey isn't sure he heard the king correctly.

"*My* name? *Mickey*? But then I'll be erasing myself! I'll disappear."

"Or you could possibly write *me*," muses the king. "If you use the third person, some other Mickey might disappear. *Me*, on the other hand, could only be you."

"Well, either way, it's crazy," says Mickey. "Why would you want me to do that? Isn't there anything else?"

"No, that's not right either, is it?" says the king, ignoring him. "Because today I declared *You are the new me*. So the Anti-Book might think *me*-meaning-*you* meant *me*-meaning-*me*!"

The king grins. His grin looks very familiar to Mickey.

"Which one of us would go? It's so confusing, I think the book might explode. What!!!"

He laughs. The laugh is familiar too.

Mickey stares. "Shadow?"

Standing, the king flings off his cape. "Surprise!"

He grabs one end of his mustache and peels off his face like a Halloween mask, revealing Shadow's face underneath.

Mickey notices that Shadow looks more solid than ever.

part five:

sad

40.

A scurry of squirrels!

"Did you know a group of squirrels is called a *scurry*?"

Smiling cheerfully, Shadow leads Mickey down a long subterranean tunnel. The king's—that is, Shadow's—entourage of squirrels surrounds Mickey on all sides.

"A scurry of squirrels!" Shadow nudges the nearest squirrel with his foot. "Must be because you're always scurrying away from me, right, squirrel-dude?"

"Right, Your Bubbleness!" squeaks the squirrel.

"I told you, you guys don't have to call me that anymore," says Shadow. "Shad is fine. Or maybe Your Shadowness, if you want to be more formal. Or Your Awesomeness—that works too. What!!!"

They are headed for Mickey's prison cell, or new "pad," as Shadow prefers to call it. Shadow has made it clear that Mickey will be kept prisoner for however long it takes for him to change his mind and write his name in the Anti-Book.

So far, Mickey has not changed his mind.

The tunnels are damp and sticky and filled with a rumbling echo that gets louder as they go deeper underground. Mickey feels as though he is inside the guts of some giant creature—a giant creature whose stomach is very, very upset.

Mickey's stomach is upset too.

Nothing in the Anti-World, he is coming to realize, is the way it seems.

Mickey thought that Shadow was his friend, or hoped he was, and all along Shadow was trying to manipulate Mickey into erasing himself.

The fact that the Bubble Gum King turned out to be Shadow only makes the betrayal stranger and harder to accept. Shadow took Mickey's fantasy and made it . . . what? Not a reality, more like a costume.

Why?

"Sorry, dude, I know it's hella gross down here," says Shadow as they tiptoe around a bubbling, tar-like pool of melted gum. "Try not to get stuck. You might never get out. Kidding. Well, no, not kidding. What!!!"

So far, Mickey has been silent during their underground journey. But now he blurts out, "Why do you hate me so much?"

"Hate you? How could I hate you?" Shadow scoffs. "I don't hate you."

"Then why do you want me to disappear so badly?"

Shadow looks at him in surprise. "You mean you don't get it yet?"

"Get what?" asks Mickey.

"Uh, how do I explain?" Shadow scratches his forehead. "Remember when you asked me what I foreshadowed, and who I was the anti-of, and all that junk?"

"Yeah, you said, *If I told you I'd have to kill you.*"

"Well . . ." Shadow looks meaningfully at Mickey.

"You were joking, right?"

"Here, look . . ." Shadow points to the bubbling pool at their feet.

"At the melted gum?"

"No, our reflections."

Mickey looks. "I can't even tell you're invisible anymore."

"I'm still not totally filled in, but that's not the point. What else do you see?"

Mickey looks again. He breathes in sharply.

How did he not see it before?

Was it that Shadow is so much paler than Mickey? That Shadow's eyes are gray while Mickey's are brown? That his hair is light rather than dark?

Because in other respects, their reflections are nearly identical.

They have the same nose (largish) and the same chin (square-ish). They have the same height (short-ish) and the same posture (slouching-ish).

Shadow even has the same annoying gap between his two front teeth.

He might as well be Mickey's twin.

Except for his personality, of course. And that has always been the most visible part of Mickey's invisible friend.

His coolness. His confidence. His jocularity.

Also, it turns out, his cruelness. His arrogance. His total heartlessness.

Mickey never thought he had any of these traits, not even the bad ones.

But maybe they were inside him all along, if only as hopes or fears about what he might someday become.

He had concentrated so much on their differences, on the many ways that this shadowy boy outshined him, it never occurred to him to look for similarities.

"Now do you see what I'm the foreshadow of?" Shadow asks.

Mickey nods. Slowly.

"That's why you always seemed so familiar. You're the foreshadow of the Anti-Me. You're the Anti-Mickey. You're what happens after . . . after I erase myself."

"Yes! You got it! The brass ring!" Excited, Shadow punches the air.

"Is that why you keep looking more solid?" Mickey asks as he follows Shadow deeper into the mountain. "Is it because . . ." He falters, unsure he wants to know the answer. "Is it because I'm getting closer to writing my name in the Anti-Book?"

"Yup. But cheer up, dude. Don't you see? You won't really be erasing yourself. You'll just become me. Like His Bubble-ness says . . ." Shadow adopts the king's voice: "*I am the new you.*"

He laughs, as though speaking like the king is a hilarious joke—and not something he was doing in earnest only a few moments ago.

Without a word, the squirrels open a heavy, padlocked door and lead Mickey into a large underground storage room filled with piles and piles of pinkish debris.

"Wouldn't you *like* to be me?" Shadow persists, standing in the doorway. "You have to admit I'm a little cooler than you are. Well, a lot cooler. And let's face it, way more handsome."

"We look the same," says Mickey.

(It's not much of a defense, but it's something.)

"Not true," says Shadow. "Looks are ninety percent confidence. And confidence is what *I* have and *you* don't."

"Is that supposed to convince me?"

"Yes! Because what's mine is yours. We will rule the Anti-World together. You and me . . . as me!"

As the door clangs behind him, Shadow tells Mickey to take some time to mull things over.

"Think about it, dude. It's the opportunity of a lifetime! Total coolness and total powerfulness in one package. I promise you, *I* will be an awesome *you*."

"What about the Anti-Book?" Mickey asks. "Can I have it back while I'm thinking?"

"Nah," says Shadow, through the grill in the door. "I'd better keep it for now."

He walks away, leaving a squirrel outside the door to guard it.

Alone in his prison cell, Mickey leans back against the wall, then slides to the floor, all willpower leaving his body.

Slumped over, he stares at his compass, which is still attached to his belt loop. The needle has moved again. It's now pointing to *S*.

S for *Sad*.

41.

Erasers.

Glumly, Mickey stares at the many piles of pink junk that fill the room.

Leftovers, he assumes, from the gum-making process. Or, at the other end of the gum lifecycle, chewed pieces of gum, hardening into rocks.

He grabs a few pieces to inspect.

Up close, they don't look like scraps *or* chewed gum. They look like people. And assorted buildings and objects.

"Hey, what are these little action figures for?" he asks the squirrel on the other side of the door. "Are they tokens for games, or prizes or something?"

"Prizes?" repeats the squirrel with a snort. "What kind of a nutcase puts a squirrel in charge of a giveaway? Ever met a squirrel before? We're hoarders, pal."

"Well, what are these things, then?"

"They're erasers."

Mickey can hear the squirrel scrambling up the side of the door until he's looking in through the grate.

"Old wads of gum. Recycled. Or is it upcycled . . . ?" The squirrel scratches his nose with a claw. "It's about sustainability, right? The environment? And no tree hugger jokes! I've heard 'em all."

Mickey can't tell whether he's being serious or sarcastic.

"So if I tried to erase a word with one, would it work?"

The squirrel chuckles. "No. No. We only call 'em erasers because each one is some unlucky sucker from your world who got erased."

"Who *I* erased, you mean?" Mickey absorbs this idea for a moment. "But they're not Anti-People?"

"Not yet anyhow. Enough chitchat," says the squirrel, disappearing from view. "The boss won't like me consorting with prisoners."

Mickey looks again at the erasers in his hand.

Upon careful examination, he sees that one resembles his math teacher, another his school's nurse. There is also a building that looks very much like the school gym. And, randomly, there is a wheelbarrow, a top hat, and a sewing thimble. He must have written something about board games in the Anti-Book.

If Mickey understands the squirrel correctly, each eraser will eventually become an Anti-Person or Anti-Thing of some sort.

For now, they're statues. Little statues. Cast in pink.

He lines up the six erasers in a row and picks up another handful.

One of the new erasers is a man holding a mug. He has a short beard and an irritated expression that Mickey recognizes immediately. Mickey is certain that if he had a magnifying glass, he would discover that the mug is decorated with emojis.

So is this where his parents have been all this time? Hidden in a pile of pink action figures?

He fishes around for several minutes. Sure enough, he finds a woman wearing hiking boots, a bandanna, and a big smile.

He stands her up next to his father.

"Hi, Dad. Hi, Mom," he says softly.

He waits, but his parents don't answer.

It's almost unbearable to look at them like this, frozen in miniature. He's glad his sister can't see them.

Over the next half hour or so, Mickey assembles a collection of erasers that includes not just his parents but most of his other relatives, and a large percentage of the population of his school, as well.

Something in one of the eraser piles catches his eye. It looks like an upside-down horse, with four legs sticking up. But when Mickey turns it over, he sees the horn on its head.

It's a unicorn. The Gender Unicorn. Or the Soon-to-Be Anti–Gender Unicorn.

The cartoonish smile and the rainbow stripes, now all shades of pink, give it away.

Mickey has been fighting it for a long time, but now, at last, as he holds the unicorn tightly in his fist, a tear rolls down his cheek.

Then another and another. Until he is sobbing.

Here, all around him, is the proof. His entire world is gone. From his mother's hiking boots to the embarrassing fantasy animal on his father's classroom wall.

And he has no one but himself to blame. He erased it all.

What kind of person would do something like that?

No wonder his father wanted to replace Mickey with a new, improved model.

Maybe he should take Shadow up on his offer, and write *Mickey* in the Anti-Book. Like Shadow says, Shadow would make a much more awesome Mickey than Mickey.

Anybody would make a more awesome Mickey than Mickey.

Funny, he told everyone else to get lost, when what he really wanted was to get lost himself.

To un-feel all those mad, sad, bad feelings. To forget the unforgettable loss of his father, of his family, of his home.

Well, he got lost in the end, didn't he? Problem is, he took the whole world with him.

And his feelings, they only got madder, sadder, and badder.

As he looks for something to wipe his nose with, Mickey hears a familiar sound in his ear.

Bzzzz.

"Felicity!"

Never in his life has Mickey been so glad to see someone.

"Yes! I'm sorry it took me so long to find you," the flyhouse says breathlessly. "It's lucky houses are so little. Otherwise, I could never have squeezed through that grate."

"I agree, houses rock—especially little flying ones!" Mickey says, smiling through his tears. "I'm really glad to see you."

"Well, thank you. I'm glad to see you too."

If it were possible to hug a little flying house, Mickey would hug Felicity now. He settles for letting her land on his arm.

"Let me catch my breath," Felicity says. "Then we've both got to fly. Or in your case, run. Your sister is in a very perilous position. Luckily, Adam tipped me off as to her whereabouts. That mime was trying to warn us about Shadow all along."

"But how am I going to get out of here?" Mickey asks. "I'm locked in."

"Ahhhhhhh . . ."

"Ahhhhhhh, what?"

"Ahhhhhhh . . . ." the flyhouse continues, her front-door mouth wide open.

"Ahhhhhhh, like you're trying to come up with a plan, but you can't? Ahhhhhhh, like you're doing a vocal exercise? Ahhhhhhh, like *Aw, shucks*?"

"No, you nincompoop!" says the flyhouse, exasperated. "Ahhhhhhh, like you're at the dentist! Ahhhhhhh, like 'Look in my mouth when I say, Ahhhhhhh!'"

As Felicity holds her front door open again, Mickey peers inside.

"Wow! Where'd you get that?" he asks, impressed.

Lying against the teeny-tiny staircase in Felicity's teeny-tiny entry hall is a teeny-tiny key. Gingerly, Mickey reaches inside and takes it.

"Oh, thank goodness!" exclaims Felicity, coughing. "That key was making me gag . . . I stole it from the squirrel, of course. He was dozing. Now, please, let's—I believe the word is *hustle*."

"Hey, is someone in there with you?" It's the squirrel, peering through the grate.

"I guess he's up now!" whispers Felicity, hiding behind Mickey.

"Sorry!" says Mickey to the squirrel. "Just talking to myself. Being locked up will do that to you, right?"

"Tell me about it," says the squirrel. "Try sitting alone in a tree for a day or two. Your mind starts playing tricks."

Inspired, Mickey picks up an eraser from his collection—a tree—and pushes it through the grate in the door. "Here— for you. Give it to your kids or something."

"Huh," says Mickey's jailer, dropping down to the floor to examine the eraser. "Looks like my old house."

The eraser distracts him just long enough for Mickey to unlock the door.

"You'll see a few more trees if you look in here," says Mickey.

As the confused squirrel steps into the jail cell, Mickey closes the door on him.

"Hey, you trying to make a chump out of me?" yells the squirrel.

"No, a chipmunk!" responds Mickey, running down the hall after Felicity.

In one pocket are his parents; in the other, the unicorn.

42.

Escape and rescue.

Felicity leads Mickey through a maze of passageways, buzzing frantically in his ear.

"Shadow is keeping Alice in a birdcage! Like a pet! Can you believe it? The cage is hanging in the sunroom. (Although where is the sun, I ask you!) I can fly to her, of course, and offer words of comfort, but what else can I do? Beneath the cage, those horrible cats are prowling around. They keep looking at Alice and licking their lips! It's only a matter of time before they devour her limb by limb!"

"Great," says Mickey. "Thank you for that image."

"I'm sorry! I just can't stop imagining the worst. You two are like children to me, you know."

The problem, as Felicity sees it, is that there are too many cats for Mickey to take on by himself. "Sure, you're bigger than they are, but they have claws," she reminds him. "And teeth! Sharp ones!"

As they debate the best course of action, Mickey hears muffled barking. Noodle!

Still muzzled, the golden dog is leashed to a column. From the looks of it, he has been trying to escape but has only succeeded in tying himself in knots.

He growls into his muzzle when he sees Mickey, as if to say, *Look what you did to me!*

"Felicity, this is Noodle, Noodle, Felicity," Mickey says, trying to untie the dog as quickly as he can.

Felicity hovers in front of the dog's glistening nose, giggling girlishly. "I can't tell you how delighted I am to meet you, Noodle! Has Mickey told you? I am a huge fan. I just adore your work."

The dog tilts his head quizzically as his muzzle comes off. "My work?"

"Your golden gifts," says Mickey.

"Oh!" says Noodle, finally stepping free of his leash. "Well, I'm glad *somebody* appreciates me."

Now that they have a third partner working with them, Mickey and Felicity waste no time coming up with a plan.

It goes like this:

Snarling like a rabid beast, Noodle tears into the sunroom, terrifying the cats.

As hoped, the cats dart off, leaving the birdcage unguarded.

Mickey runs in, pulls a chair from the side of the room, stands on it, and unlatches the cage.

He finds his sister sitting atop a T-style bird stand. She swings off like a gymnast and lands in his hand.

"Thanks."

"No problem."

He gives his sister a quick kiss on the head, and slips her into his sweatshirt pocket.

Another second, and he's at the door.

They are *this* close to escaping.

But then:

Shadow appears out of nowhere to block Mickey's exit. There are squirrels at Shadow's feet and on his shoulders, all baring their teeth and holding needle-size swords.

Mickey looks behind, but the other doors are closed.

The cats have returned. They hiss at the squirrels.

For a brief, hopeful second, Mickey thinks a battle might break out between the two groups of animals, but no such luck. Shadow signals with his hand and the animals quiet down at once.

"Big props for that escape and rescue, bro," says Shadow. "I didn't think you had it in you."

"Well, I had some help," admits Mickey.

He gives a thumbs-up to Felicity, who is flying as close to Shadow's face as she dares, and to Noodle, who is standing at Mickey's side, growling at Shadow.

For her part, Alice gives Shadow the stink eye from Mickey's sweatshirt pocket.

Shadow takes them all in with a smirk. "You guys need

to work on your 'band of rebels' vibe. Maybe bandannas? Or freedom fighter T-shirts?"

"Let us go and we'll get them," says Alice. "We'll even send you one."

Shadow points at her. "Did your brave brother tell you I offered to save you? All he has to do is write his name in the Anti-Book. But he's too scared and too selfish to try."

"If you're telling him to, it's a trap," says Alice fiercely. "Don't do it, Mickey."

"Sorry, little sis, but it's your only option," says Shadow. "Neither of us has the power to get you home on our own."

Frowning, Alice looks up at her brother. "Is that true?"

"I don't know," says Mickey. "Maybe."

"I'm going to give you guys time to talk it over," says Shadow. "Sign the book or rot in cages. The choice is yours."

He puts two fingers in his mouth and whistles.

"Troops!" he says, addressing the cats and the squirrels. "Everyone out! Let's give these kids some privacy."

Grumbling angrily, the animals stare at Mickey, then follow Shadow out without a word.

Mickey watches, miserable, as the door closes behind them.

"Sorry, I messed up, guys," he says after a moment. "Shadow's a creep. I should have known. And it's worse than you think . . ."

Mickey starts to tell them about writing the list in the Anti-Book, about how he is responsible for everything that has happened.

"Stop," says his sister before he can get very far. "I figured it out already."

Mickey looks at her, stricken. "Aren't you mad at me?"

"Yes. But it's done. And I forgive you."

"Me too," says Noodle. "Even though I don't know what she's talking about. No worries, man."

Sitting upright, the dog thumps his chest with his paw. "Best friends forever."

"Really?" says Mickey. "Even though I throw away your poops? Even though I tried to use you to rescue my sister?"

"Even though."

"What about when I don't walk you when I say I will?"

"It's okay, I get it," says Noodle. "Humans are like cats. Sometimes you need to be alone."

"I thought you didn't like cats."

"I don't . . . But I love you anyway." He nudges Mickey's leg.

"Why?" asks Mickey, wanting to believe it, but unable to. "Why would you love somebody like me?"

"Oh, stop it!" says Felicity. "What kind of question is that?"

The dog nods in agreement. "Love doesn't have reasons. Love is love."

"Noodle's right," says Alice. "I'm your sister. I don't need a reason to love you."

"Yeah, but maybe I need to *hear* a reason."

"Okay," says Alice. "How about the fact that you just rushed in here to rescue me, knowing you'd probably get caught? Or the fact that you're smart and caring and always make me laugh? Or the fact that you let me have all the Pegasuses even though you wanted them?"

"You said that was so I wouldn't fly off a table again and kill myself."

"Wellllll," Alice admits, "it might also, just possibly, have been because I liked Pegasuses better than unicorns."

"I knew it! You are such a . . . big sister."

They both laugh.

"Okay to pick you up?" Mickey asks.

"Yep."

Mickey lifts his sister out of his pocket and cups her in his hand—closest he can get to giving her a hug.

"Hey, give me some of that!" says Noodle.

Mickey puts his arm over the dog. The dog licks away his tears.

"Oh, this is so sweet, I can hardly stand it," declares Felicity, who is bobbing in the air, her windows foggy from crying.

"Wait, I have an idea," says Mickey, pulling himself together.

It'll either get us all home or it will be the end of me, he thinks.

Before any of the others can stop him, he strides over to the open doorway and beckons to a passing squirrel. "Hey, guard! Tell Shadow to bring the Anti-Book. I'm ready to write my name."

43.

Any last goodbyes?

He could pass for a normal, un-see-through, completely solid boy, Mickey thinks when Shadow returns.

There's a soft glow where the light still comes through, and a certain fuzziness around the edges. But not so as you'd notice if you weren't looking for it.

"I promise, Mickey, you won't regret this." Shadow smiles paternally, like he did when he was the Bubble Gum King. His tone of voice is suddenly more mature as well. "Think of it this way: You're taking one for the team."

Mickey nods. "I'm trying."

"I'm proud of you. Any last goodbyes?"

At this, muffled gasps can be heard from Alice, Felicity, and Noodle.

"Nope, that's all done," says Mickey.

"No, it's not!" cries Felicity. "I will never be done saying goodbye to you, Mickey!"

The flyhouse hovers in front of Mickey's nose, her windows awash in tears. "There must be another way . . ."

"I will always be saying goodbye to you too," Mickey whispers, giving her a little, flyhouse-size smile. "But there's no other way."

Choking back a sob, Felicity turns and flies to Alice and Noodle.

"Is that it?" says Shadow, unable to hide his impatience.

He hands the Anti-Book to Mickey, as well as the small, almost-but-not-quite-used-up pencil that has somehow made it all this way.

"I sharpened the pencil for you."

"Thanks."

Mickey turns the Anti-Book over in his hand. It feels like a long time since he last wrote in it, though it's only been a few hours.

"Are you going to write *Mickey* or *me*?" asks Shadow. He's so full of nervous excitement that he is starting to pace. "I think *Mickey* might work better in the end. Yeah. *Mickey*. Definitely."

"Okay," says Mickey. "*Mickey* it is."

He rests the Anti-Book on top of the back of a chair and opens it.

With his free hand, he gives the little unicorn in his pants pocket a squeeze for good luck.

"Okay," he repeats.

Then—with the whole room holding its breath, and

with Shadow looking over his shoulder—he puts pencil to paper and starts to write:

S-H-A-D-

"What the—? No!!!!"
Shadow reaches for the pencil, but he's too late.

O-W

When Mickey finishes writing Shadow's name, he looks up at Shadow and sees *himself* standing there, glaring at him. But it's not a better self. Not a more awesome self. Maybe not even a cooler or a better-looking self.

It's Mickey's worst self because it's the self that tells him that he's worthless. That to be someone he must be someone else.

"You think you can get rid of me that easily?" Shadow says, laughing scornfully. "Every test that you fail. Every game that you lose. Every lunch that you eat alone . . ." He taps his forehead. "I'll be right here. Every time."

"Well then, I'll just have to write your name every time, won't I?" says Mickey.

Furious, Shadow raises a fist, as if about to strike Mickey. Instead, he holds his fist in the air, staring at it. His hand is almost totally transparent, and his arm is not far behind.

He's turning invisible again.

While Mickey silently watches, Shadow slowly dissolves.

Until, at the moment he's about to disappear altogether, the room starts to dissolve as well.

Thrown backward, Mickey falls to the floor, only to discover that the floor is spinning.

In a fraction of a second, he is slipping feet-first into what looks very much like the top of a tornado.

44.

G.

Mickey has no idea how much time has passed when he lifts his head, but he knows immediately where he is. If the gravel under his butt isn't enough to tell him, there's the sign standing in front of him:

BASKETBALL TONIGHT:
ARROYO PERDIDO VS MESA MIDDLE
GO CHOLLAS!

Mickey moves his arms and legs experimentally. He's sore, but uninjured.

From inside his school, a bell rings twice. Kids start to holler. It's recess.

Mickey rises shakily to his feet.

His sister and dog are nowhere to be seen. But he's not

worried. He feels sure somehow that they are safe. He'll see them later.

First stop: the cafeteria. He wants a carton of milk.

As he walks into school, his little plastic compass swings from his belt loop. If anybody bothered to look, they'd see that it isn't pointing in any of the usual directions.

It's pointing to *G*.

Glad.

part six:
glad

45.

Dad.

Not that day, nor the next day, nor the day after that, but fairly soon, no more than a week or two or three later at most, Mickey screws up the courage to confront his father.

They meet in the counselor's office, but Mickey makes it clear he's talking to his father as his father, not as his counselor, and definitely not as his Human Development teacher.

Even though the first thing Mickey mentions took place in his father's class.

"Remember that day I kept popping bubbles? Well, I guess it's kind of obvious, but yeah, I think I was mad at you."

As plainly as he can without choking up, he repeats what he overheard the night he slept at his father's house.

About him.

Sorry about Mickey . . .

And about his father wanting a new family.

I just want to start all over . . .

Then, and this part is even harder, Mickey tells his father that hearing him say these things made him feel like there was something wrong with him.

That it made him worry that his father thought of him the same way Car-Boy and the kids at school did.

That it made him think that his parents' divorce was his fault.

There is a painful silence.

"That was very brave of you, telling me all that," his father says finally.

Mickey nods, uncomfortable, but grateful for the acknowledgment.

"Now listen to me, Mickey. Because this is important. There is nothing wrong with you. Nothing. I love you exactly the way you are."

Mickey's father, when Mickey can bring himself to look him in the face, has tears in his eyes. So does Mickey.

"I don't want to change you. And I would never, ever want to replace you."

"You wouldn't?" Mickey's voice catches.

"No. Of course not. Come here."

His father wraps him in a hug.

"I'm really sorry you heard all that. And I'm even

sorrier that I said it. I was frustrated, but that's no excuse."

"Well, in your defense, I was kind of a jerk about the cookies," says Mickey.

"Yeah, you were," says his dad. "But in *your* defense, divorce stinks."

"Yeah, it does."

Mickey pulls away from his father and unzips his backpack.

"I want to show you something. It's a list. Kind of."

He takes out a notebook and opens it on his father's desk. It's not the Anti-Book, but it's about the same size. He bought it very recently.

"Remember you told me to write a thank-you note to the world?"

His father puts on a pair of reading glasses and holds Mickey's notebook up to the light.

"*Why I love donuts—because, duh, donuts,*" his father reads. "*Why I love my dog—because there doesn't have to be a reason to love a dog. Why I love my sister—because she's my sister, and also because Pegasuses are cool, but unicorns are cool too. Why I love my dad—because when I was little, he used to spin me around, and he never stopped until I told him to, even though he must have been very dizzy . . .*"

Mickey's dad smiles. "I remember that—it did make me dizzy! This is a great thank-you note to the world, Mickey. Thank you for including me in it."

He looks down at the notebook again. "There must be at least a hundred things you love in here, but it looks like you're missing one."

"What's that?" Mickeys asks, genuinely curious.

"You. I think you ought to write down what you love about yourself."

Mickey reddens. "Oh, right. That's . . ."

"Not easy? You'll come up with something. You have a way with words, always have. That's one of the things *I* love about you . . . Do you still make up names for everyone?"

"Well, not *every*one."

"I've always thought you might become a writer one day. Did you know I wanted to be a writer when I was younger?"

"You did?"

"Yep. I've got a couple of half-written, and more than half-horrible, novels in a drawer somewhere. Maybe I can live out all my dreams through you. Now *there's* a healthy father-son relationship!" He laughs.

Mickey doesn't join in. He's still thinking about what his father just suggested.

A writer? Him?

Of what kind of book?

Any kind, he answers for himself. As long as it's a *book* book. Not an anti-book.

A week later Mickey finds the letter that has been slipped into his backpack.

It's another list. All the things Mickey's father loves about Mickey. There's a ton of them.

Plus extra lines for Mickey to fill in.

46.

Mom.

Mickey's mother is surprised that Mickey has started staying over at his father's house a few nights a week. But she's even more surprised when he proposes that they go on one of their old veggie-oil supply runs in her car, which she notices he no longer refers to as the Pee-ew Wagon.

It's monsoon season, and before they've driven very far, a heavy rain crashes down on them out of nowhere, as it does in the desert.

They have to roll up the windows, and it gets humid inside the car pretty quickly. For a while, they both do a good job of pretending not to mind the smell, but eventually they start to giggle. It smells so rancid that it would be impossible for anyone to ignore.

As soon as the rain slows, mother and son simultaneously roll down their windows, stick their heads out of the car, and gulp the desert air.

"Don't you just love the smell of the desert after a rain?" asks Mickey's mother, sighing, when her head is back inside.

"Yeah, I always forget how great it is," says Mickey sincerely. "It's the mesquite. And the creosote. And the sand, I guess?"

"Right. But it also means mosquitoes," says his mother. "Let's go."

Later, when they arrive home, before they get out of the car, she turns to Mickey and asks, "Was there something you wanted to talk about? Is that why you wanted to go on a drive?"

"No," says Mickey. "I just missed you. That's all."

"Me too." His mother leans over and gives him a kiss. "You're a really great kid when you want to be. And even when you don't."

They are interrupted by barks.

Noodle, acting like a puppy, is running and jumping all over the driveway, trying to remove the unicorn horn and Pegasus wings that are tied to him. Alice, meanwhile, watches from the door of the house, laughing hysterically.

"I found our old costumes," she said.

"Yeah, I can see that," says Mickey.

"What do you say we dye him rainbow tonight?"

"Can we start with maybe just one color?"

"Boring!"

"So. I have some news," she tells Mickey, following him into his bedroom. "I broke up with Sean today."

"Oh," says Mickey carefully.

As far as he can tell, his sister has no memories of the Anti-World. But sometimes it seems like she has absorbed its lessons all the same.

"That's it? Aren't you psyched? I thought you hated him."

"I am. I do. I was just trying not to gloat."

"Gloat! Gloat already! You deserve to gloat. I demand that you gloat. You were right about him all along. I don't know what I saw in him."

Mickey smirks. "His muscles?"

"Besides his muscles," says Alice, blushing. "And, by the way, I don't like the way he uses the word *gay* all the time. As a dis."

Mickey looks at his sister. This is the conversation he has been avoiding. For reasons he can't quite explain.

"Me neither."

Alice picks a thread off the side of her sweats. Mickey knows she is looking at him without looking at him.

"I especially don't like it when he says it to you."

"You mean like every time he's ever talked to me?"

"Yeah." Alice winces. "Sorry about that. I just didn't hear it. I mean, I heard it but I didn't *hear* it."

She looks at Mickey. Finally. She really is sorry. He can tell.

"Apology accepted."

"Cool. So now that that's all out of the way . . ." says Alice, treading very gently. "*Are* you . . . gay?"

"No," Mickey answers reflexively, then hesitates. "And if I am, it's because I am. Not because somebody calls me that."

"Of course."

"It's *my* thing," Mickey insists. "Or not. Either way, it's mine."

"Agree one thousand percent."

"Same if I'm bi or trans or just . . . whatever I am."

"Totally."

"Okay then."

"Okay then."

Silence.

Mickey looks back down at the thread Alice is still picking off her pants leg. "But say I was . . . gay, would it be okay with you?"

"Are you kidding?" Alice practically shouts. "It would be the bomb. You could be my brother *and* my gay best friend! I mean, think about it. We could have our own social media channels, and we could do makeovers and stuff together, and be influencers and get sponsors and move to L.A. and—"

"Calm down!" Mickey says.

She grabs him, pleading. "Oh, please, please be gay!"

"Hold on." Now Mickey is laughing. "You know that's not how it works. First of all, not *all* gay people do makeovers. Some are mechanics or whatever. Plus, I told you. If I *am* gay, it's not going to be because someone tells me to be. Not even you."

"Fine, fine," says Alice, pouting. "But can I at least dye your hair pink tonight?"

"Sure, I guess."

"Or rainbow?" She grins. "You and Noodle will match!"

Mickey tries not to grin back, but it's useless.

Especially since Noodle has walked in, looking very disgruntled. Somehow, the unicorn horn has ended up on his back, and the wings on his head.

A rainbow dye job is just what the veterinarian ordered.

Epilogue

Now, I don't want you to think Mickey is an entirely new person these days. He's not all rainbows and sunshine. Sure, he smiles sometimes, but not *all* the time. Not even most of the time. Mickey is still Mickey.

Take Chrismukkah, for example.

Their family mega-holiday was a record twenty days straight with no break this year.

The first time they all got together—Mickey, Alice, Mom, Dad, Charlie, and Charlie—it was, as Alice put it, "über-awkward." The second time, it was much easier, almost familial, which was, Mickey agreed, "über-cringey."

With four parents, a teenage sister, an aging dog, two kinds of chocolate chip cookies, and endless charades, Mickey got increasingly cranky, and started pantomiming obnoxious and borderline inappropriate messages instead of movie titles. (See: *typical behavior of twelve-year-old male*.) Sure, it was nice that everyone made the attempt to get into the family spirit, but he was more than ready for it to be over when it was over.

What else?

He's going through a black T-shirt/blue hair phase (and not washing either enough, according to his sister). People at school have been telling him he's "emo," or that he's an "eboy," or just that he's "e." He doesn't think he is, but whatever. Those are labels he can live with, until he finds his own. It's kind of funny when you think about it. *Emo* is short for *emotional*—the very thing Mickey was fighting so hard not to be.

He still gets pelted with basketballs now and then. But he has learned to throw them back. Sometimes he has even managed to pelt the pelter, so to speak.

Luckily, Alice was right: He's a fast runner.

There are still plenty of things that irritate him. Including things that come without batteries, the Copy Cats, and, *Sorry, Noodle!*, picking up his dog's poop. (Some things never get easier.)

Add to the list: gum.

He has totally lost the taste for it. Bubble-gum flavor especially. Just the thought of it makes him ill.

He has fantasized about writing *gum* in the Anti-Book, but he knows it would be unfair to all the people who still love gum. Besides, it seems like a slippery slope. If he erased gum from the world, what might he erase next?

He has been keeping the Anti-Book under his bed, for lack of anywhere better to put it. He knows he has to get rid of it eventually. It is too much of a temptation, sitting there. But he is afraid to throw it away. You never know who might pick it up. Or what havoc they might wreak if they did.

His most recent idea: Write the name of the Anti-Book in the Anti-Book. Presumably, the book will vanish as soon as he does so. A perfect solution.

So why hasn't he done it yet?

For one, he is afraid that it won't work, and that he'll discover that the book isn't magic. That he dreamed the whole thing. Which is what he told Alice the one time he dared mention the Anti-World to her. That it was all a dream. (If she'd had the same dream, she didn't say so.)

Then again, the alternative is much worse. Because if the book disappears, his memory of it likely will too. And he can't bear the thought that he might forget the worst, but also best, and certainly weirdest, thing that ever happened to him.

It will take him weeks to solve this particular puzzle. But when he does, the answer will seem obvious.

Yes, words may be erased, but if he has learned anything from the Anti-Book, it's that they never fully go away.

What should he do if he wants to remember what happened? What should anyone do?

Write it down.

And so, Mickey starts reliving his Anti-adventures. He writes day after day—not in the Anti-Book, or even in a

notebook, but, if you must know, on a boring old MacBook—
until he has recorded everything he remembers.

Then, late one night, after saying a final goodbye to
the flyhouse and the scrime and Shadow and the rest,
Mickey closes his computer and pulls the Anti-Book out
from under his bed.

It's now or never, he tells himself, opening it.

A-N-T-I-, he writes with the shortest of possible pencils.

Then *B-O-O-*

Acknowledgments

When I first thought of the idea, nearly ten years ago, of a book that makes an unhappy boy's world disappear, I didn't imagine that *The Anti-Book* would debut in a world that is *actually* disappearing. And yet, here we are. As I write these words, schools like Mickey's lie empty, and shops like Desert Donut stay closed. By the time *The Anti-Book* reaches store shelves, the COVID pandemic will—hopefully—be receding. But the enormity of the loss will still be with us, as will, no doubt, much of the rage and despair.

These feelings can be overwhelming for anyone, but especially for kids. My hope is that Mickey's story will provide a safe—and fun—way for young readers to explore the emotional darkness.

Writing *The Anti-Book* was far from easy, not least because it is the first book I've written under my own name. Many times, feeling exposed, I considered abandoning the project altogether. But one person always had faith: my agent, Sarah Burnes. From the moment I told her the title, she insisted that *The Anti-Book* was the book that I had to write. I wasn't always certain what she saw in it, or in me, but her certainty was enough. Thank you, Sarah.

Perhaps the hardest thing about an empty world is choosing what to put in it. Luckily, I had an expert guide as I mapped the Anti-World's desert landscape. Like all great editors, Lauri Hornik didn't tell me what she wanted for my book so much as help me figure out what *I* wanted. Huge thanks to Lauri and her team at Dial—including, among many others, Michelle Lee for the close read, Jennifer Kelly for the book's interior design, and Theresa Evangelista for her patience as I gave multiple conflicting notes about the book's cover.

The talented artist behind that cover, as well as the book's interior art? A bike-riding bloke named Ben Scruton. For more of Ben's sometimes wacky, always wonderful illustrations, check out www.ben-scruton.com.

As I stumbled my way through *The Anti-Book,* many friends, fellow writers, and family members cheered me, counseled me, and chided me, as necessary. A big, socially distant hug to Margaret Stohl, Hilary Reyl, Michael Ravitch, Shane Pangburn, Melissa de la Cruz, Carter Elwood, Roxana Tynan, Nicole de Leon, Jason Hoover, Jesse Simon, Sara Newkirk-Simon, and, of course, my mother and eternal writing mentor, Dyanne Asimow.

At twelve, my daughters, India and Natalia, feel they are too old for my books. (They're not!) Nonetheless, they graciously consented to read *The Anti-Book* and even to give me notes. As did their other father, my husband and occasional partner-in-creative-crime, Phillip de Leon. Thank you, family, for the help. But mostly thank you for the love that makes a book worth writing—and a life worth living—even in the bleakest of times.